The Fortune Teller's Garden

The Fortune Teller's Garden

Frances DeleCourt Winters

Black Lyon Publishing, LLC

THE FORTUNE TELLER'S GARDEN
Copyright © 2014 by Frances DeleCourt Winters

Our books may be ordered through your local bookstore or by
visiting the publisher:

www.BlackLyonPublishing.com

Black Lyon Publishing, LLC
PO Box 567
Baker City, OR 97814

This is a work of fiction. All of the characters, names, events,
organizations and conversations in this novel are either the products
of the author's vivid imagination or are used in a fictitious way for the
purposes of this story.

ISBN-10:   1-934912-68-9
ISBN-13: 978-1-934912-68-3
Library of Congress Control Number: 2014950746

Published and printed in the United States of America.

Black Lyon Contemporary Romance

To Rich Stockwell: The most romantic story of my life.

Chapter 1

She sold hope. Her clients came to her for security and solace, and left with comfort and a soul warmed from her signature tea. (Her grandmother's original recipe). The faded sign out front, however, told a different story. Withered and splintered with age, it appeared lost among the raggedy catnip and wild daisies that grew unfettered under the gaze of the sprawling old porch. Her loyal clients acknowledged the sign's presence with comfortable familiarity and always looked for it—not for its instruction, but for the simple recognition of an old friend who has withstood as many seasons as they.

Fortunes Told, it read.

Painted in powder blue on an old shutter, Keighley's grandmother, Hattie, added a cobweb in the corner with a whimsical spider dangling from a thread over the letter D. Thirty years later, that cobweb and spider looked more like a distant memory than the actual artist's hand.

Keighley was twenty-six. She read palms and doled out gentle advice based upon her observations. She wasn't psychic. She was simply observant and carried on her grandmother's tradition in the very parlor her grandmother had used. Hattie kept a crystal ball on the center of the dark maple table adorned by two tall candles, and truly convinced her clients that her special gifts and polished crystal ball could reveal their futures.

In truth, like her grandmother before her, Keighley's powers were simply based on a sharp eye, keen observations and a healthy dose of kindness.

Though the rest of the old house was in need of repair, Keighley did her best to keep the parlor looking the way her grandmother had, with a few minor adjustments that only time can create. The dark oaken floors that once reflected spectacular amber light from frequent beeswax polishings, now seemed to absorb that light and held onto it selfishly, as if craving its warmth. If you looked closely, you could see the dried yellowed tape her grandmother used to join the seams of ancient peeling wallpaper, and the ruby velvet curtains that draped the tall windows had faded a bit. As sun bleached caresses gave away their true age, the drapes absorbed the parlor's confidential conversations and held their secrets like a wise sentinel holding court.

Keighley looked softly at the old woman sitting across from her. They had just finished a reading.

Cradling the old woman's hand in her palms, Keighley began. "It's okay to be angry with someone who has passed and still have room to love them." She sought recognition in the woman's eyes.

Mrs. Sylvane was weeping softly and released her fingers from Keighley's warm hand. She dotted her aged, damp cheeks with an embroidered kerchief, and looked at the young, wise woman she visited once a week.

"I know that dear," she responded. "The house has just become so quiet with him gone. I didn't know what quiet was until Harry passed." She paused a moment. "I think that's why I'm so angry. How am I supposed to fill up all that silence?" She sighed.

Keighley knew her job well. "You fill that silence with the sound of your heart," she said, touching the old woman's hands, whose skin was so thin it looked like tissue paper. "Mrs. Sylvane, you were married for over half a century. My generation can only dream of a romance like yours. They don't exist anymore. My friends don't believe in a romance like that. Mr. Sylvane loved you immensely, and your heart still resonates with that love. Let it beat loudly." She smiled. "And hopefully the rest of us will be able to hear it. There's great healing there," she said. Keighley's smile soon warmed them both.

Mrs. Sylvane studied that smile and let the glow surround her for a moment. She marveled at how one so young was so insightful and wise. *Must be her grandmother's touch*, she thought.

She sighed and changed the subject. "How's your grandfather doing?" she asked. "He's such a dear man." The whole town knew Albert's gentle nature, and those who were lucky enough had one of his paintings gracing their home. He was known for his slightly modernist style, landscapes and gardens with an abundance of purples and greens, lines and angles that never quite met, yet viewed as a whole, they formed a riotous dance of joy.

Keighley smiled at her friend's kind question. "He's fine. He has his good days and some slow ones too. You know how it is. He's slowed down a bit, but we read each other well. We're good company."

Keighley had cared for her grandfather, and since his mild stroke last year, she refused to believe he could be declining. Truth is, he was getting slower and a bit more difficult to care for. Mrs. Sylvane could see Keighley looked a bit more tired than usual.

"Keighley dear," she said. "Now I hope I'm not out of line and it's none of my business, but this house is too quiet." She gave Keighley a motherly smile with a familiar raised eyebrow. "A nice young girl like you? Why you should have a string of admirers! When are you going to let a nice young man into your life? Why, young men should be lining up on your porch."

"I doubt that old porch would stand all that weight," she laughed. "Besides, I'm a lot to take on. Who'd want a fortune teller and a house held together with tape and glue?" She paused. "No, Mrs. Sylvane. It's not in my cards. I'm fine the way things are. Just me, my Pop-Pop, and my cat." She feigned her confidence and hoped her old friend didn't notice. "Now, how about that cup of tea?" Keighley prodded, eyebrows raised, hoping to change the subject. Mrs. Sylvane smiled broadly. This was her favorite part of her weekly rituals to the fortune teller's parlor. "Child," she said, "that cup of tea may be just what the doctor ordered. And it's high time you started calling me Ruth."

Keighley's tea was known throughout Cobweb

Corners.

Indeed, it may have been the real reason she was so well liked by her clients. Once the palm was read and the fortune was told, Keighley set out Hattie's ancient Staffordshire tea set and poured them both a cup of hot tea. Keighley still used Hattie's tea recipe made from herbs and flowers she picked herself in the tea garden out back and sweetened it with a touch of local honey. The delicate tea cups were so thin, the flowers adorning each cup seemed to glow with colorful translucent light from within each petal. As the steam rose, the fragrance of lavender and chamomile haunted the air of the old parlor, and the two ladies settled into their respective armchairs and talked.

Well … Mrs. Sylvane talked and Keighley smiled as she listened to her old friend's chatter about the Cobweb Corners of her past. As each memory was spoken, Ruth's sorrow was momentarily lifted and carried away in the sweetly scented air.

At twenty six, Keighley was alone in the world except for her grandfather and large tabby cat, Ginger. She never knew her parents. They died tragically the week she was born. An icy road on a dark night took them away and she was instantly whisked to her grandparents' house in Cobweb Corners, New Hampshire. The tall, three-story Victorian house stood in the center of the small bay town. With its slender windows and splintered angles, it could easily be the town's haunted house if it weren't so beautiful.

Keighley's grandfather, Albert, made sure his home was the pride of the community. He kept the lawn tightly groomed and every other year or so, the ornate trim and gables were painted in complimentary tones of honey ambers and cool fern greens. From the third floor, its center gable gave a romantic view of the entire seaside town laid out like a worn patchwork quilt, and on clear nights, one could see the distant lighthouse, proclaiming its serenity with romantic grace.

Below, the house solidly met the earth as though it had earned its strength through the passing centuries and intended to keep its position. The wrap-around porch that once invited visitors to sit for a spell and share news and local gossip, was in need of repair. Railings were cracked, and a few missing spindles gave the viewer impression of a warm smile missing a few teeth. Meeting the rickety porch steps was an overgrown stone path that led friends around back to an exploding herb garden. Shaped like a large carriage wheel, mounds of catmint, fennel, chamomile, sage and lavender grew riotously like spidery cupcakes.

The house would have been admired even more if it weren't for that silly sign of Hattie's. Aided by her stubbornly gentle insistence, Albert made it from an old shutter he found in the attic and leftover bucket of blue paint. *Just to keep her happy*, he thought. *Fortunes Told*, it read. He had his hobby, painting, and she needed hers. But fortune telling? In a town like Cobweb Corners? Hattie's nutty idea couldn't last that long. *Sheesh, I must be outta my mind* he thought as he watched his wife happily paint a spider web on the upper corner of the sign.

ॐ

Though most of Keighley's clientele were elderly locals, from time to time she would get the occasional stray. The wife who feared her husband's infidelity and sat nervously as Keighley revealed the heartbreak in her young client's eyes, or the occasional frat boy looking for a good laugh—and left, shamed, head over heels in love with Keighley's natural beauty and grace. Each session lasted about forty-five minutes, and at twenty-five dollars, most left feeling it was money well spent.

Her regulars knew the crystal ball she kept on the table belonged Hattie and was for looks only, though none of them said as much. They were there, true, to have their fortunes told. But what most of them were really after was to simply spend time in Keighley's good graces. It was her gentle palms they sought, not the palm reading. It was the delightful conversation over that cup of tea, not the tea leaves, that they felt was Keighley's greatest gift. And when the palm reading was over, and the invitation to tea arrived, many of her clients sighed in anticipation of the pleasure of Keighley's sweet tea, the comfortable chair, and the opportunity to relive old memories with this kind young woman.

"Well dear," Mrs. Sylvane said, gingerly setting her tea cup on its saucer, "I've taken up enough of your time." As she reached into her faded purse to retrieve Keighley's payment, the young woman patted her hand and smiled.

"Not this time, Mrs. Sylvane," she said kindly. "Today's reading was on me."

Keighley, though low on funds this week, was paid in kind by the smile that grew on Ruth Sylvane's face.

"You're such a dear," the old woman replied. "I'll bring you a jar of those peach preserves I put up last week, maybe even two." And with that, Mrs. Sylvane patted Keigley's young face with her dry hands and smiled at this kind young woman whose insight was so sincere, and she was out the door.

"Give your grandfather my best," she waved, hollering over her shoulder.

Keighley watched as Mrs. Sylvane descended the porch steps and delicately made her way along the old stone path to the driveway, her tiny feet nearly obliterated among the many flowers and herbs that spilled over the flagstone and threatened to take over the yard.

Ginger was weaving in and out of the catnip, purring mightily, enjoying the early spring sun. She gave this friendly visitor a gentle meow, and Keighley laughed at the sight. Ginger quickly looked up, surprised by Keighley's laugh.

"C'mon girl!" Keighley called. Ginger darted up the rough porch steps, curled around Keighley's legs for a moment, and like lightening, disappeared into the house to seek one of the many deep windowsills favored by this morning's sunlight.

As Keighley was putting away the tea set, she heard a knock on the old front door. Wiping her hands on her jeans, she headed down the hallway and called out, "Did you forget something, Mrs. Sylvane?"

She opened the heavy oak door and took a breath, for standing merely three feet away was the most handsome young man she had ever seen. His square, firm jaw was dusted with a tawny shadow of finely trimmed beard.

His thick lips had the faintest hint of a smile, and though hidden under a baseball cap, she looked into his brown eyes, deep as an autumn forest.

Chapter 2

His breath caught in his throat. When the door flew open, he was totally caught off guard. He wasn't expecting her to be so young. In his experience with fortune tellers, he was used to middle-aged women who looked a bit worn out with cynicism and age. But this girl? She looked like she just stepped from the pages of a natural shampoo ad or a commercial for healthy foods, organic living and sparkling water. Embarrassed, he found he was stammering.

"I'm um. I ah … Um, fortune teller?" he was unable to find the words. "Telling! I'm here for my fortune told. Wait," he said, embarrassed and attempting to breathe. "Let me start again?"

Leaning against the door jam, she folded her arms and smiled at the handsome stranger.

He took a deep breath and began. "My name's Connor Jakes. I saw your sign," he took another breath, "and I'd like my fortune told."

"Ohhh," she replied. Enchanted by this man's nervous energy, she was charmed to have been the cause.

"Well, c'mon in," she said. "My name's Keighley Woodson. I just finished with a client, so you'll have to wait in the hall while I prepare the parlor. It'll only take a minute."

She beckoned him inside and her friendly gaze reassured him that he was indeed welcome. He followed her into the old home, which smelled sweetly of lavender and honey. The wide hallway floor squeaked in protest under his weight, crying from the unfamiliar step of this young healthy man walking over its surface.

"Have a seat right here and I'll be with you right away," she said. "Pop-Pop," she yelled down the hall, "I have another client, so I'll be with you in a half hour or so, okay?"

A simple muffled response was received, and Keighley knew she could begin.

She looked at this young man. His shyness seemed innocent enough. "Go on," she coaxed, "have a seat. I'll be right with you."

Entranced, he watched her as she disappeared behind the curtain that sealed off the parlor. He sat on the dark hall bench and under confused dark brows, he thought in silence.

There was something about this young woman he recognized. He tried to search his memory for the connection. It wasn't her face that was familiar. She was so pretty, he'd remember that face anywhere. No. It was something altogether different. Just looking at her, being near her felt comforting, sincere and true. He tried to resist the stirring inside. She wasn't like an acquaintance or an old flame, but something more elemental, more familiar. And the fact that she was beautiful simply added to his racing heartbeat.

He took a deep breath, shook off the thought, and looked around the large hallway. Seemed typical for a house of its era. The dark paneled walls were haunted by faded red wallpaper, and the hallway receded into foreign distant rooms. A large staircase loomed to the right, its creaky banister worn from a million hands. He looked across from his seat. A series of oddly colorful paintings graced the shadowy wall. Garden statues and nudes, lonely interiors and brilliant landscapes were all heavily framed in carved waves of tarnished silver and oak. They seemed to dance in the dimly lit space. Yet it was the table opposite him that held his attention. He spent a few moments looking at it.

"My inheritance," Keighley noted.

"Huh? What?" he replied, surprised she was standing there. He hadn't heard her return.

"I see you found my inheritance," Keighley laughed. She was leaning against the doorway, watching this new stranger absorb her unique home.

"Uh, yeah," he said, "that thing must weight a thousand

pounds." He wondered how the old table, with legs spindly as carved carrot sticks withstood its weighty occupant.

He was looking at an ancient glass jug. Huge. It stood about two and a half feet high, and just about as wide. Its sheer weight dominated the hallway. It sat like an ancient, fat god proclaiming its space. Its dusty surface appeared to be made of smoky copper-toned glass, but once his eyes adjusted to the dim hallway light, he noticed it was filled with pennies, thousands and thousands of pennies.

"There must be a couple hundred bucks in there," he told her, awed by the sight.

"My grandfather has been adding pennies to that jug since the day he married my grandmother," Keighley explained.

He listened closely to her voice. It warmed him. It was smooth as vanilla silk, soft as amber, smoky like whiskey.

And the paintings?" he asked.

"Some are mine, some are my grandfather's," she said simply.

"You're an artist?" She became more intriguing by the moment.

"We both are. He doesn't paint much anymore. I guess I got my painting style from him, and the palm reading from my grandmother," she explained.

He looked more closely at the paintings on the long wall. There must have been at least twenty of them in a mass of different sizes. Some large as a table, others small as a saucer. He tried to avoid staring too long at several nudes. Though stylized and abstracted a bit, they were still nudes and he felt embarrassed to gaze too long.

He turned to her. "You live with your grandparents?" he asked. He was curious, sure. But he'd ask her to recite the phone book at this point. Anything to keep her talking just so he could listen to that voice.

"Just my grandpa," Keighley explained. "My grandmother died about ten years ago. She was a fortune teller too. But now it's just me, my Pop-Pop, and my cat." Keighley laughed. She glanced at the floor and shook her head slightly. She suddenly realized how eccentric her life sounded.

She looked at him, searching his face for a sign of

recognition. She moved a step closer and noticed his square, rugged shoulders, his firm jaw, which hinted of a soft shadow of scruff, those brown puppy eyes, which seemed hungry for comfort. As she moved closer, she smiled inwardly at his quick intake of breath.

Was he nervous?

She tried to relax this handsome stranger.

She gave a gentle dusting across the heavy jar. "My grandfather always told me there was nothing lower than a penny. If the stock market crashed again, these pennies would be worth their weight in gold." She laughed. "Trouble is, the jug is too heavy to move, and too delicate to tip. It would shatter from the weight. And that jug? May be worth more than the cash inside. So there it sits, impossible to use, but pretty to look at."

He wasn't sure if she were talking about the jug, or herself. He tried to suppress his curiosity about her and found he was failing, big time. He swore off relationships over two years ago and for the first time in ages, he felt the emptiness of his current life.

"Well, shall we get started?" she asked. She held open the curtain and invited him in.

Chapter 3

He wasn't prepared for the warmth. The entire room seemed to glow in an amber hue and he wasn't sure if it came from the lights, the window, or Keighley herself. Sure, the room looked used. The floor was dusted with scratches and footfalls from a century of wear, but what struck him was the fact that the room felt sincere—not at all like the other fortune tellers he had visited, whose fake parlors were just props used to support a sideshow performance. Nothing here was out of place or reeked of cheap beads and gaudy scarves.

The light was soft. The wood was worn smooth, and the air smelled sweetly, like a memory of Christmases past.

"So, have a seat at the table, and we can get started," she requested. "Would you remove your cap? It's still my grandmother's parlor."

Besides, I need to see those brown eyes again, she thought and smiled to herself.

"I charge twenty-five dollars for a reading. It'll last about half an hour and comes with a follow-up analysis of your reading and some fresh tea from the garden. How's that sound?"

"Fine," he responded. "Though I'm not a tea kinda guy."

"We'll see," she said easily.

He sat down at the small round table and noticed the traditional crystal ball in the center. It reflected the entire room in exaggerated curves and inflated colors. The effect was dizzying.

Keighley lit two tall baby-blue candles on the table and moved the crystal ball to the deep windowsill where it gathered sunlight and warmed itself.

"No crystal ball?" he asked.

"No, that was my grandmother's style," she responded. "My grandmother told fortunes in this room for years. She used the crystal ball, tarot cards, that kind of thing. I have a bit more basic, hands-on style." She smiled. "I read palms."

She sat down across from him.

"Now, before we begin, I just need to clear the space a bit, okay? Give me your hands?"

He gulped. Perhaps too loudly. He reached across the table and between the lit candles, placed his hands into her open palms, hoping she wouldn't notice he was trembling.

Though her hands were soft, the slight calluses gave evidence that this woman was not unaccustomed to hard work. They cradled his own and with great relief, he felt the heat travel straight to his core. Had it been that long? He tried to ignore her slight stroking as her fingers met his rough palm.

Stop! he told himself. Agitated, he tried to shake off any thought of joy and comfort, women and soft skin. Distracted, he tried to focus on the task at hand.

The fortune teller was watching him.

Was she smiling?

Or was that a flirt?

Or just simple curiosity?

"Connor," she said reassuringly, "this works better if you close your eyes for a moment and try to clear your brain. I'm sensing a lot of activity going on in there." She smiled.

Oh man, you don't know the half of it, he joked to himself.

So he closed his eyes. He took a deep breath and let it out, slowly.

"That's it," she reassured. "Just relax and quiet your thoughts for a moment."

So the two strangers sat silently at the small table for a moment or two, hands linked. The house slowly settled around them, took a breath, and it, too, found its past was calmed by the presence of these two strangers momentarily united in the amber glow of candlelight.

"Okay, that's great," she said slowly, and released his sturdy hands.

The spell was broken.

The air was suddenly normal again and Connor, opening his eyes, found himself disappointed to return to the world of sunlight.

"Let me see your right hand?" she requested.

He held out his hand, palm up, and she cupped it in both of her palms.

"I read palms," she told him. "Your life history, your internal struggles, your external strengths, all of them are written on the skin of our hands. The wrinkles in your palms," she explained, "are like road maps of our lives." She tapped the center of his palm. The sensation went straight to his core, bypassing his brain, his logic, his limitations. "Where we've been, what we carry, what we need to let go of and what we should embrace. It's all there."

She noticed his eyes. Brown and soft, like a gentle cub's, they receded under furrowed brows, yet there was also a distant sorrow surrounding them. They receded too far.

She took note.

"Okay, let's begin." She pointed to the wrinkle that curved along the top of his palm. "This line here?" She tapped it. "This is the heart line. It reveals your emotional side, your experiences in love." She studied it intently for a few moments. Flexing his palm in the warm light, she noticed his hands were strong and firm with slightly rougher spots at the fingertips. She followed the curve and thought a moment. She made a few mental notes and hummed a little.

She moved on. "This second line, just below? It's the head line. It's like an I.D. card for your accumulated knowledge, life lessons, school, that kind of thing."

Keighley was remarkably natural. The tacky parlor tricks he was used to from other psychics was missing. Instead, Keighley's parlor seemed to manufacture its own light, natural and clear, the way sun reflects off of water. It danced through the air and surrounded him.

He was entranced.

Slightly tracing the line in his palm with her fingertip, he flinched a bit. The slight smile on the side of his full lips betrayed him. He was enamored by her touch and welcomed her silken fingertip on his palm. He prayed she didn't notice.

She did.

So did he.

They smiled briefly at each other, shyly acknowledging the moment they had just shared—and she began again.

"Your head line slopes across your palm. You're a creative man aren't you, Mr. Jakes?"

Before he could reply, she continued. "Also, the line is very deep and doesn't meet your life line, just below it. Not only are you creative, but you're pretty insightful and adventurous too." She paused a moment and looked at him, those eyes. "You like a good adventure, huh?" she laughed. She could see this guy could be fun, but there was a distance to him. There was a protective armor surrounding him and she couldn't quite nail what it was.

She broke away from his eyes and looked at his palm again. Her grip tightened a bit as she tapped a point on his vulnerable open hand. "This cross," she said, "this small line that intersects your head line … " She didn't finish the sentence. What she saw was troubling. She studied it deeply, tapping his palm as she thought. She traced the other paths she followed to this line and decided to put her discoveries aside for a moment.

"Your life line is strong and healthy. It's deep," she said. "See how it curves in this broad swoop? That shows that you're a strong guy with a lot of enthusiasm for a life well-lived. You like your friends, it's clear. You're a good friend, too," she told him.

"So far," he said, surprised he found his voice, "that's all pretty basic, don't you think? Can't you give me anything more substantial, more personal?" He was used to the same old generalities from self-proclaimed fortune tellers.

Slightly challenged by his call, Keighley continued. Without guile or mean-spiritedness, she told him, "Well, clearly there's been some emotional trauma in your past." She didn't need to read his palm to see that. Keighley noticed it in his face right away.

He stiffened slightly.

She pointed to his heart line. "See these small creases across your heart line? It's all right there. Somewhere along the line, you suffered a great loss. Also, there is a small line across your head line as well. That's another indicator of a sorrowful experience somewhere in the past. Perhaps some depression too?"

"We all have that," he said.

"Mr. Jakes, clearly there's something troubling you from your past. It looks pretty deep too. Very deep." She looked at him, trying to read if he was truly listening. It was hard to tell. "However, right here?" She tapped gently. "This is good. Your life line meets your fate line right in the center. Something good may be in the horizon. Your palm is telling you that you may need to surrender a bit in order to move on."

"Move on from what?" His tone was slightly defensive.

Keighley took a cleansing breath and began gently. "You're carrying around a heavy weight. There is damage here. But there is also a journey of healing. You are a creative, life-loving, and affirmative man but something stopped that. There is a loss in your past, suffering that you carry with you still."

He paled slightly and averted his eyes.

Instantly taking his hand from her warm palm, he replied, suddenly stoic, "I don't know what you're talking about," and with that, he shut down. Keighley could see he was no longer responsive. Within seconds, he seemed to surround himself with a thick coat of protective armor. Though he sat there as real as a mighty soldier ready for battle, his eyes revealed the profound loss of a frightened child.

"That's okay," she reassured him. She studied him quietly for a moment. She decided not to continue. He looked too hurt. "How about I make us some tea? Try it if you want to, and we can take a walk through the herb garden out back. Many people find it very relaxing after a reading."

"Naw, that's okay," he said, anxious to leave, but also, hungry to stay. "What do I owe you? Twenty-five dollars you said?" He stood and took out his worn leather wallet, and grabbed his cap.

"That's right," she said. She could see she hit a nerve and this man was hurting for an escape route. She tried again. "How about a walk through the halls? I can show you our paintings, some of them can be a little crazy, but you're a creative guy.

I can tell. There's a callous on your index finger—are you a writer?"

He stopped shuffling through his wallet and froze. He looked at her deeply, softly, and for a moment he looked like a pony ready to bolt.

"Um, yeah," he said, fumbling with his wallet. "Something like that," he managed to say. He found the cash and handed it to her, anxious to avoid her eyes. "Here ya go. Thanks for the reading." He tried to sound stable, but inside he was shaking like an old shutter in a terrible storm.

"That's fine," she reassured, concerned by this young man's sudden change in demeanor. "Here, take my card. If you ever want to come back, just make an appointment. It's easy. I'll walk you to the door," she offered.

"I'm fine," he said firmly. "I can find my way out," and with that, he pocketed her card and walked through the curtained doorway. She listened to his heavy footsteps in the hall. Very heavy. She expected to hear the front door slam and braced herself for the blow.

Nothing.

She walked closer to the parlor doorway and listened. Surprised, she heard the old oak door swing closed, gently. Its lock rested back in its place with a soft click, and the strange man's gentle footsteps disappeared along the garden path.

The house was suddenly silent again.

Ordinary.

A muffled call from the back room. Pop-Pop.

"Keighley," it called in a soft voice and worn from time. "The pennies," it called weakly. "Did you find the pennies?"

She turned. "Yes, Pop-Pop," she replied patiently. Lately, he had become obsessed about the penny jar. "They're right here in the hallway," she reassured him. "They've always been right here."

He continued to mumble softly to himself, and waited for Keighley's return.

And with that, she blew out the candles, took a cleansing breath, and went to care for her grandfather.

Chapter 4

"Connor, dude! Are you listening? Man, you're a million miles away!" Brian was rattling his empty scotch glass at a waitress when he noticed Connor was no longer there in spirit.

"Sorry, Brian. I'm still a little shook up. This chick was something else." Connor took a long pull from his beer and glanced around the bar, trying to gather his thoughts. Walden's Pub was busy tonight. The twang of a popular country song rattled from the old speakers and a noisy crowd added to the heady scent of burgers and ale. No wonder he was having trouble focusing. "She wasn't at all like the others. There was something different about this one." He paused and tried to ignore the memory of her eyes, soft as a fawn's.

"What? No black cat? No missing teeth? Dude, you're weeks behind on the article and I need to see some progress here," Brian told him firmly.

Brian Vicks was the editor of *The Road Less Traveled,* a trendy New England bi-monthly magazine that explored the unique, the off-beat and the eccentric side of New England living. He was currently trying to convince one of his best writers to pick up the pace.

"Connor, when you proposed the idea of an article on these phony psychics, I thought it was perfect, really. But man," he said, "it was perfect last Halloween. Let's get a move on, okay?"

Connor took another long slug from his beer. "Yeah, sorry, Brian," he said. "Let me try to get an interview or two from her this week, and I'll have the article done by the end of the month. I swear."

"Good, I can live with that. But no longer than a month, or I gotta scrap the idea. October will be here before you know it." Brian was a fair but firm editor and appreciated Connor's work. He'd known Connor for five years and could always count on him for a solid, well-written story. He knew the past two years had been difficult for Connor, yet he never let his demand for content be swayed by his sympathy for his friend.

"So, how's it going?" Brian asked, suddenly cheered by the arrival of his second scotch.

"Good. It's going good," Connor replied, attempting to sound more confident than he was. His afternoon with Keighley still rang in his mind. "I've got the historical research done. The Fox sisters, Houdini's attempts, Lilydale New York, all that stuff. Some sideshow tricks, too. I compiled the interviews from the other fortune tellers last week. Now, a few more interviews with today's subject and I'm ready to go. This info is so easy, it'll practically write itself," he said easily. He took a swig and gulped, deeply.

So why do I suddenly feel so guilty?

He took the last long pull from his bottle and pushed the thought aside. Raising his empty toward the passing waitress, he signaled for another brew. She smiled at Connor and winked. He was used to random flirtations like this. He felted warmed by it, and, as always, shrugged it off.

Brian saw the wink and laughed. "My friend," he said, cautiously approaching the topic, "it may be time to get back into the ring again. It's been two years, ya know?" He held Connor's eyes. "Randy would want that. She wouldn't want you to be alone."

Connor looked down at his empty beer and said nothing.

Brian stood and gulped down the remains of his second scotch in a single swig, thought about offering his lonely friend a last bit of friendly advice, and decided against it. He knew when to back off.

"Well, I'm outta here," he said, putting on his coat. "Look, you're a good writer, better than what this magazine needs." He tossed a twenty on the table. "Get the article to me by the end of the month, and I'll see about throwing something bigger your way," he offered.

Connor nodded. "Cool. Thanks," he said. "I'll keep in touch and get you a draft next week."

"That's m'man," Brian encouraged. And with that, he disappeared in the crowded pub.

Connor sat alone at the table.

The music suddenly seemed louder and the pub appeared more crowded.

Staring at his empty bottle, he tried to ignore the peeled corner of the label he had nervously scratched off during the conversation with his boss. He truly liked Brian. Even though there was only a five-year difference in their age, Brian tried to pull the father-knows-best routine too often. Though he'd really come through for Connor two years ago. When Connor's life suddenly inhaled a tragedy he thought he'd never recover from, Brian helped him reassemble the pieces back into something that resembled normalcy.

He sighed.

"Here's that beer, handsome."

He jumped. The waitress set the cold beer on the table and moving a small wad of chewing gum to the back of her mouth, she asked happily, "Anything else I can get cha?"

She waited.

"No. No, that's it. Just the check," he told her with an animated smile. Giving him a slight shrug, she moved on.

He reached into his pocket and felt its presence. Still there. Firm in shape, he grasped it tightly his hand and felt it melt into the shape of his damp palm. It felt good.

Keighley's business card.

It had burned in his pocket all night long. Like a glowing key, he was aware of its presence, but unable to decipher its meaning.

He took a long pull from his fresh beer and looked at the card.

It was simple enough. Soft green text on a rich purple background, *Fortunes Told*, it read. Trimmed in winding flowers, the only gothic element may have been the small spider dangling over the letter D. Other than that, it may have read, *Wedding Photography* or *Child Care*. It was that innocent.

There was a phone number on the bottom.

The previous psychics and fortune tellers he'd visited were adorned with an abundance of tacky symbols and gimmicks. Dusty parlors decorated with vintage posters of palms and crystal balls, table lamps covered in silken kerchiefs, dozens of half-melted candles the color of blood, gypsy women in brightly colored turbans, beaded doorways, vintage ouija boards—the works. One young woman even had the nerve to seductively say, "Come into my parlor said the spider to the fly," as she invited him through her bead covered doorway. She beckoned with a soft pale finger and nails the color of a poisoned apple. He had to suppress his urge to laugh.

But Keighley was different.

He knew this.

Knew it.

And he couldn't get her out of his mind.

Nine months ago, he approached Brian with an idea for an article exposing the tricks of fortune tellers. He got the notion from watching an old movie about Houdini starring Tony Curtis. It unnerved him that people actually charged money to offer assurance on their futures and the afterlife. And that jazz about talking with dead loved ones? That's what threw him over the edge. Charlatans who abused the tragedy of others. Even more, he was angered that people actually believed in this garbage.

Brain accepted the story idea immediately and Connor got to work. The first five fortune tellers he visited and interviewed were easy targets. He'd show up for a fortune telling, then contact them the day after about an interview for *The Road Less Traveled*. All except one were eager for the publicity and though Connor never mentioned his article's actual tone to them, he did make it clear he was a non-believer.

But Keighley?

She was different. She seemed more sincere than the others. His half-hour with her lacked the performance, the trickery, the guile that he found so infuriating.

So why do I feel so guilty?

He quickly dismissed the thought. He tossed a ten on the table and made his way through the crowded pub to the door.

"See ya, handsome," the waitress called. He smiled back at

her and reached the door.

When he stood outside, he found himself finally able to breathe. The last rays of the April sun had just licked the edge of the horizon and the scent of New England pines was rich in the air. Dusk had fallen over sleepy Cobweb Corners.

He breathed deeply and sat against his car.

He looked at her card again. It had become wrinkled in his tight fist and showed more creases and life lines than his own palm. He pulled out his cell phone and dialed.

A message machine.

"Hi, Keighley," he said, pleased at how calm he sounded. "This is Connor Jakes from this afternoon? I'm wondering if we can meet again. You see, I'm writing an article and …"

He left a brief message with his cell number as the sound of evening crickets erupted in a scolding chorus around him.

So why do I feel so guilty …

Chapter 5

He arrived the next morning, more excited to see Keighley than the prospects of actually finishing his article. Her house was partially visible from the quiet street. Its bottom story was hidden by the lusty overgrowth and numerous pines and maples that surrounded her property. Parting the wild shrubs and overgrown hedges, the unpaved driveway was bordered by two craggy stone pillars. One boasted the address on a cast iron plate. *1111 Pynchon Farm Road* it read in Olde English type. Must have cost a bundle in its day.

Her house rose in front of him. Tall and thin, it looked as if it was pushed out of the very earth, stretching its wiry, shuttered gables toward the warmth of the sun, appearing as if, it too, had grown out of the fertile soil of its surroundings. Nothing here looked out of place, yet each glance, each vision gave the uninitiated viewer the idea that order and control where lost to the centuries.

The stone path to the porch was so overgrown it cried for a good pair of clippers, and he quickly noticed the lawn needed a mowing. Looking at her house, he saw the chimneys needed pointing and the house was desperate for a good coat of paint. Half a dozen shutters had twisted from their hinges as well. They hung at odd angles like the sleepy eyes of an old hound dog, aware of a predator, but too lazy to bark.

She said she'd be in the garden. He parked the car and followed the path to the back the house.

Why do I suddenly feel like the big bad wolf?

Turning the corner, he faced the garden. His heart leapt into his throat. There she was, kneeling in one of the concentric paths of the herb garden, pulling weeds among mounds of silvery leaves in the fresh morning air. Enrapt, he watched as she abstractedly whisked away a strand of hair that stubbornly refused to stay behind her ear. This gesture, so simple, so graceful, suddenly filled him with a warmth he hadn't experienced in years.

Was it the sun that made her so bright? Her cotton dress? She seemed to radiate. Hoping not to be noticed, he watched as she lazily picked a few leaves off a greyish twig and rubbed them briskly in her slender hands. When she lifted her palms up to her nose, she inhaled deeply. She smiled at the scent and softened as she held it in her lungs for a moment. He noticed a large orange cat had curled around her knees, and with a smile and a sigh, she exhaled and got back to the task at hand.

He longed to sit by her, to bathe in the scent of her long hair, the color of glowing wheat. He wanted to know what it would be like to hold her scent in his lungs the way she inhaled those leaves, like a forgotten lover. He wanted to know a smile like that again, to release his own inhibitions that grew from his years of drought. Watching her was like watching the rain. Gentle, cleansing, and desired.

He didn't want to be seen. He wanted this silence to continue for eternity. As long as he could gaze upon this beautiful young woman, absorbed in her work, he was happy.

He noticed that.

For the first time in two years, he suddenly felt happy.

Maybe Brian was right.

ભ

"Lavender," she called out over her shoulder. Without looking up, she knew he was there. She felt his presence the moment he arrived. Plus, he slammed his car door just like a guy. Too hard. Too firm. Too loud—even the birds took flight. She laughed and shook her head. What were these guys trying to prove?

She looked up at him and noticed his distance. He stood at the far edge of the herb garden like he was afraid to enter its circle without a proper invitation.

"I love the smell of lavender," she said laughing. "Come here and try it."

He entered her garden.

The better to smell you with my dear.

The sudden flair of guilt rose in his chest and he tried to suppress it.

"How do I get to you?" he asked, puzzled by the choices of paths in front of him. "Which path do I take?" He laughed at the maze in front of him.

"They all lead to the same place," she encouraged. "Doesn't matter which path, but watch those roses on your left, they have killer thorns," she shouted. She noticed he seemed to be walking as if he were on a sheet of ice, unsure of the ground beneath his feet. She smiled at this solid man, so unused to garden paths. The car-door slammer seemed to disappear and was replaced by a shy puppy.

Or a clever wolf.

She had a hard time judging this handsome stranger.

The garden was huge, fertile, and damp. It gave the impression it had no beginning or end. Just endless circular pathways that meandered through a riot of color. He followed a path through the garden and arrived in the center, where she stood.

She was wearing a simple white cotton dress that stopped just below the knee. It was dusted with a few grass clippings, and a random leaf clung to its surface here and there. He laughed aloud at how natural she was. He knew he was seeing the image of pure peace and longed to be in its glow.

She ran her fingers swiftly along a stalk of lavender, and rubbed the slender leaves together in her palms.

"Here," she offered, "take a deep breath."

He smiled, broadly, somewhat embarrassed. "What?" he replied, fearful she'd notice his nervous attraction to her.

"Go on," she said happily. "It smells wonderful. Take a deep breath."

As she held her palms up to his face, she noticed his racing pulse. She saw his eyes, darting everywhere but at her. Daring him to look at her, she held her gaze and waited, patiently.

Connor's heart was pounding. What was it about her that made him so nervous and so comfortable? So riotous and so calm? Fearfully, he leaned forward and took a deep breath and held onto it.

Deeply.

He wanted to grab her hands, to press his face into her palms, to feel her soft white skin press against his cheeks, his brow, his lips.

He wasn't sure if the scent he held inside was the strange herb, or some deeply recessed spring emanating from Keighley herself. His brain was lost in the heady scent and he felt like he was about to explode. All of his pains and joys seemed to ignite together in one illuminated flame. Language was light years away.

"Nice," was all he could muster. "That's nice."

Good God, he thought. *She must think I'm such a smack! What kind of idiot says nice?* He prayed he could muster the strength to calm his mind and actually talk to the woman.

What is it about her?

☃

"So, you're writing an article, huh?" she began. "I figured there was something up. I don't usually get drop-ins like you."

"Like me?" he said. He was still reaching to form words. For a writer, his words usually came easily. But around Keighley? Language became foreign, words clogged in his throat like oil on felt. "What d'ya mean? You see it in the cards or something?" he tried joking and actually managed a natural laugh.

She smiled in return.

"No," she replied, tapping his chest. "When you arrived, you said you saw my sign. That thing hasn't been visible from the road in years." She was on to him. "So, I figured you heard about me from someone in town, or a buddy perhaps." She hoped it was the former. The locals liked her.

She gazed up at this sturdy man with the ruggedly handsome face. *Sculpted bronze*, she thought as she glanced at his muscular arms. His strong neck rose from broad shoulders, which looked as though they had been carrying a burden too heavy for one so young. She figured he was somewhere around twenty-eight? Thirty-two? Somewhere in there.

His square jaw was firm, and when he laughed, she noticed his smile was full and rich. It raised his deep eyes so they were warmed from the sun.

Brown as a puppy's, she thought. *Or deep as a wolf's.*

"So?" she asked. "Have a seat." She was acutely aware of his broad chest and tapered waist as he looked around for a chair. He noticed there were none when she suddenly plunked herself on the ground, gathering her white dress around her. "What this article all about?" she asked.

He was unaccustomed to sitting on the raw earth, but not uncomfortable. He sat and watched her fingers stroke the weedy grass as he spoke.

"I'm writing an article on fortune tellers and psychics— their history, the job, that kind of thing."

He buried the truth deep in the earth below him.

"I've been traveling around New England. Visiting fortune tellers, getting readings, following them up with interviews. It's been pretty good too. Only one refused me so far," he smiled. "I'm hoping you won't be number two." A touch of a smile grazed his generous lips.

"Who do you write for?" she asked.

"*The Road Less Traveled,*" he replied. When he told her the name of the magazine, he felt encouraged by her reply.

"I know that magazine." She laughed. "People with houses made from coke bottles, haunted graveyards, old ladies with a hundred cats. Thanks for including me in that list," she said jokingly. Her face lit up as she laughed. Realistically, she knew this article could boost business, and lately, she needed all the business she could get.

She looked at him, deeply, and smiled. She decided to trust him. "Tell me more."

"Well," he responded. "It comes out six times a year. We have a subscription base of over ..."

"Stop!" she laughed. "I didn't mean about the magazine. I meant tell me more about yourself. How long have you been a writer? Do you like it?"

She smiled as he began to talk, and the morning drifted away.

He never even noticed she had turned the tables on him.

Chapter 6

"I have a hundred great opening lines for short stories," he told her. "But that's where it ends." Shadows curled lazily through the yard and neither was aware that the sun had reached its height, and noon was swiftly gliding away.

"So you never got through a whole story? A bit of a novel?" she asked him. She was enjoying the conversation. He had a tough exterior, but through this one simple crack, Keighley saw a flicker of warmth buried beneath those rough jeans and T-shirt.

"I have a ton of half-started stories," he replied. "It's just completing them that's hard. I used to want to write fiction more than anything. In college. I wanted that perfect writer's desk, ya know? Next to a window with a view of the ocean." He laughed at the memory. "Write the great American novel, that kind of thing. Then the job with Brian came along and I snagged it."

"What else do you do?" she asked. From the way he looked at her paintings yesterday, she could tell there was a creative spirit locked away in there.

"Now?" he asked, pleased by her attention. "I mainly write for Brian's magazine. I do a couple other articles here and there. Nothing big, no short stories, no novels." He shrugged.

She smiled at him and tilted her head a bit. "Do you think you'll ever try creative writing again? From all of your magazine articles, you must have a million stories to tell. I'll bet some are even crazier than mine."

He laughed. "No," he said shortly. "*Road Less Traveled* takes up the majority of my time. I like it, though. I meet some cool people." He held her eyes and smiled, hoping she'd return the favor.

A dry cough came from the corner of the yard and Keighley looked up quickly.

"Give me a minute?" she asked. "That's my grandfather. Be right back."

Connor watched as Keighley ran softly through the garden, gently sliding through the tall daisies and passing through the abundant roses. The thorns held no threat to her as she glided through. Any other person would have been sliced to bits by their threatening claws.

Connor stood up, wiped the grass and leaves from his pants, and watched as Keighley tended to her grandfather. Pop-Pop was sitting in an old chair in the shade, straw hat protecting his wrinkled brow, orange cat protecting his lap. As Keighley approached, Ginger stood up, gave Pop-Pop's arm a rub with her large furry head, and jumped in the grass.

"Pop-Pop, how are you doing?" she asked gently. Ginger meowed softly and Connor started to follow the path through the garden. "Would you like to go back inside? I'll fix lunch and you can watch that painting show? Remember? The one on PBS?" Connor saw the old man nod. Keighley put her arm around him to help him up and Connor saw she was struggling a bit.

"Connor?" she looked up at him. "Would you give me a hand? Sometimes we have a hard time getting started," she explained gently.

"Pop-Pop, this is Connor, the man I told you about?" She spoke a bit more loudly. "He's here to write an article about grandma Hattie and me."

The old man became more animated. A light seemed to return to his cloudy eyes as he looked up at Connor and smiled. "So," he said slowly, "you're here for my girl?" His voice sounded like sawdust on a dry desert wind but his eyes were bright and knowing. Balancing unsteadily, he held tightly to Keighley and allowed Connor's arm to aid him out of the chair and across the lawn. "Be careful of this one," he joked with the young man. "Don't let her fool ya! She's as sly as her grandma, and as pretty as her mother, too."

Connor noticed the old man's demeanor change when he mentioned Keighley's mother. He sank a bit and appeared lost for a moment, then, with a confused eye, looked at Keighley and asked, "Did you find the money? The pennies?" He seemed lost and miles away.

"Yes, Pop-Pop, we did. They're in the jug on the hall, remember?" She exchanged a concerned glance with Connor, and the moment passed.

They walked slowly. Guiding Pop-Pop through the lawn wasn't a problem once he was up. He had remarkable reserves of strength. Ginger wove expertly between their legs, mewing at the humans as they approached the back porch.

"Just help me with the stairs, Connor?" she asked quietly.

They stood behind as he pulled himself along the railing, up the five steps to the porch, each step a milestone, and each milestone, a triumph.

"I'm fine, child. I'm fine," Pop-Pop reassured his granddaughter. "I'm not an invalid." He reached out and finished the journey on his own. Keighley smiled, relieved. Lately, she had taken to mothering him too closely.

When he reached the porch door, he turned to Connor. "Young man," he said, "If you know what's good for ya, you'll make dinner reservations by Friday. This girl has to get out more!" Connor laughed at the man's gentle ribbing, and noticed Keighley blushed a bit.

"Have a seat here, Connor. I'll be right back." And with that, Keighley took her grandfather into the large home.

The old screen door banged shut behind them and Connor sat on the old porch furniture. Unsure if it would hold him, the chair looked as if it had been in use since the Taft administration. Chipped wicker, tatty legs, functional seat. However, when he sat down in the large, high-backed chair, he found that the hundreds of bodies that had worn its hide had also made it extremely comfortable and easy to get lost in. He allowed himself to relax in this large tame beast, took a deep breath, and slowly realized this was a good day.

A good day.

Was it the view of the wild yard?

Was it the welcoming spring sun?

Or was it Keighley herself?

Something was awakening inside him and he tried to keep it buried. But the warmth was a shallow burial and he secretly hoped this new feeling would resurface to the light again and again.

He smiled.

Listening closely, he could hear the distant TV turn on, the sound of silverware being set on a metal TV table, a plate, a jug, a pour. A few mumbled encouraging words.

Lunch was served.

Moments later, Keighley returned, with two tall glasses of sweet iced tea and placed them on the small wicker table beside him. Wiping her hands on the sides of her dress, she said, "Sorry to keep you—just had to get him ready for lunch. Pop-Pop suggested I bring you some tea. Now where were we?"

"Well, I came here to interview you, but somehow," he said slowly, "I got roped into talking about myself."

She smiled in return and Connor was happy to be the source.

"I think your grandfather is right. There is a sly streak in you," he joked. He tried to ignore the rising guilt over his article. "So, can we get started?"

"Aw c'mon now," she said. "If I'm giving you a story, I expect to know something about the guy whose writing it." "So," she began. "Tell me about college. Where did you—"

"Nope! My turn." He laughed, and pulled a small pad and pencil out of his pocket—and began.

Chapter 7

Keighley took a lazy sip of her iced tea, licked her lips, and looked at Connor. For the first time that day, he looked confident, comfortable. She curled up in the chair, wrapped her feet under her cotton dress, and began.

"When I was a kid, I used to love to polish my grandma's crystal ball. She swore by it," she told him. Her face lit up at the memory. "It was like this big secret world inside that ball, and I thought if I kept it polished every day, the whole world would be clean, and neat, and shiny—no worries." She smiled. "Have you ever really looked at a crystal ball? I mean really looked at one? Inside of it is like ..." She thought for a moment, smiling. "Like a fun house. Everything upside down and reversed. Distorted, too. Crazy-like." She paused for a moment, lost in that distant memory.

"What do you mean?" he asked, intrigued not only by her story, but also by the sound of her voice. Listening to her was like inhaling warm maple syrup, comforting and familiar. If he held on to it long enough, it would seep into his core and soon, he'd bleed white chocolate, joyful for the cut.

"I used to look for my mother in that ball," she confessed, holding his eyes, looking for comfort. "I'd polish it with my shirt, hold it in my small hands—and let me tell you, those things are heavy! And I'd look into it the way my grandma did. She used to stare so solidly into that thing, just off to the side, like she was in a trance. But the only thing I ever saw was my nose, magnified a hundred times like in a fun house mirror," she laughed slightly.

"Where is your mom?" he asked her, attempting to take

notes, but too distracted by her glow to concentrate on his work.

"Oh, I thought you knew. The whole town does," she replied easily. "My parents were killed a week after I was born," she told him. "A car accident."

Connor stopped writing and looked at her.

The story was easier for her to tell than it was for strangers to hear, but something about her tale rang deeply in Connor, she could tell.

"I was still in the hospital, complications or something, and they were driving home. It was icy and they hit a bad patch. I guess the car lost control and they hit a tree." She paused. "Pop-Pop tells me they died holding hands. Or, that's how the story goes anyway." She looked a Connor, deeply. "At least," she said, "I'd like to believe that's true."

She nodded a bit and smiled at this handsome young man who walked into her quiet life only yesterday, amazed she felt so comfortable talking to him. "I've lived here my whole life."

"Wow," he replied, at a loss for words. "I'm really sorry."

"Oh don't be, but thanks anyway," she said. "I never knew them. I was only a week old. But I guess it was hard on my grandparents, real hard." She stopped and asked, "But you're not here about that, are you? So! Let's move on …"

She sat forward, energized, placed her bare feet firmly on the floor, happy to change the topic for she could see it had somehow bothered Connor. He seemed to have retreated a bit.

"So! Fortune telling!" she said, happy to be back on track. Brushing her hair behind her ears, she began. "Well, I guess you can say I've grown up with the best. My grandmother, Hattie, was the best fortune teller around. People used to drive from all over just to have their fortunes told. I remember this one lady. She used to drive all the way from Peterborough New Hampshire just to see my grandma! Can you imagine? That's over three hours away. But every month, there'd she be, stepping out of this ratty VW, cigarette hanging out of her mouth, and a purse the size of a laundry bag." They both laughed at Keighley's story. "She was well-known, my grandma."

"What would she do?" he asked. "I mean your grandmother.

How did she work?"

"Well, Hattie was an old school fortune teller. She loved, and I mean *loved*, her crystal ball. She used cards sometimes too, but she said they weren't as good."

"Good?" he asked, puzzled. "What do you mean, good?"

"Well, each fortune teller, intuitive, whatever you want to call us, has their preferred method of fortune telling. Grandma loved her crystal ball, but it never worked for me. I tried, but never saw a thing. Nada. Nothing. One guy I know swears by reading tea leaves. Just looks like dirty dishwater to me." She laughed. "I showed you yesterday, I prefer reading palms. Just seems to work for me."

"Why?" he asked her. "Can you tell me how?" Somehow, he had been able to swallow the guilt about his article, locked it away deep in his gut where it burned slow and hot.

"How?" she asked, with a tilt of her head. "Well, think about your reading yesterday. How was it? Seems to me like I hit on something? Yes?" she hinted gently. "Connor, Your palm is a map of your life. Each line registers an event, an emotion, a strength. That kind of thing. Look," she said seriously, "I'm not a psychic, never claimed to be. I don't predict a thing. What I am is intuitive. I read the map on your palm, observe body language, make some suggestions and discuss the reactions. That's all. No secrets there."

She took a long sip of her cold tea, and observed this man as he took notes.

"What I am is a good listener," she told him. "I listen to what clients offer me and sew it up into a big, invisible quilt for them to examine. Generally, we explore the patterns in that quilt together and usually, the client will follow the stitches like a road, ya know? They just got lost somewhere along the line. What they discover along that road is up to them. I just hold their hand along the way. You don't need to be a fortune teller to see when someone needs a little compassion. It's not magic, Connor. It's the human heart. It's simply that some people have stopped listening to the beat. I just remind them that the beat is still there, though it may be weak. Sometimes we just have to turn up the volume." She laughed joyfully at her silly metaphor and hoped it made sense to this handsome stranger.

She looked at his hands, his long sturdy fingers, his square palms—and she realized she wanted to touch them again. She noticed how his T-shirt clung to his well-formed muscles and for the first time in years, she longed to get lost in a deep solid embrace. She noticed his shoulders, broad and firm, yet too stiff.

Perhaps that was it.

Though his voice was as comfortable and safe as her favorite flannel shirt, there was a stiffness in his body that betrayed his deep and resonant voice.

When he glanced up from his note pad, she realized she had been staring, and smiled, embarrassed to have been caught.

Connor returned the glance, just to show he noticed, and she smiled even more.

He tapped his pencil on his note pad, distractedly.

They were silent for a few moments and noticed a chorus of crickets had slowly turned up the volume. Dusk was approaching slowly over Cobweb Corners' early spring.

And they sat, silently, waiting for the other to start, and suddenly too shy to begin.

Finally, Keighley broke the silence.

"Mr. Jakes," she said in mock formality, "I'm afraid my grandfather needs me. It's time for his evening tea. Can I be of any other service to you?"

He grinned broadly, loving the time spent in her eyes.

"No, really," she said. Her smile lingered. "I do need to get inside. Can we continue this soon?"

"Sure, sure," he said, reluctant to let go of her. "I understand. Can I call you tomorrow and we can set up a time then?"

"That sounds great," Keighley replied, hoping she didn't sound too enthusiastic.

"Great," he said, "and thanks for the tea."

He was frozen to the floor. He instinctively knew he should begin walking, but his feet weren't listening to his brain.

He laughed. He saw she recognized his reluctance to go.

"Anything else?" she asked. Her dress was taking on the glow of the late afternoon sun and he noticed a single bead of sweat begin to trickle down her slim white neck, the color of cream. He longed to reach out to it. To brush it away, to graze his thumb over it, to linger there, where the bead rested upon her gentle shoulder. To taste it.

"Um, no. No, thanks for the afternoon. I'll call you tomorrow, okay?" he managed to say. Why were words becoming so difficult again?

"Connor." She looked at him and smiled. "Please do." And with that, she turned and entered the mysterious house, though her smile remained in the air long after he heard the porch door close.

He took a breath and held it deep inside, like he was holding on to the memory of her eyes, her smile, her skin. Happily, he walked back to his car, lost in his own mind and content from the journey. A hundred conflicting images ricocheted through his brain in patterns more distorted than Hattie's crystal ball. When he sat in his car, he was comforted by its familiar sag and its day-old fast food smell. Guy stuff.

He stared at his cell phone.

A message from Brian.

He pressed play and Brian's loud voice ended the sanctuary he felt all afternoon.

"Heeeey Connor Buddy!" He listened. "Just wondering how that interview went! Call me and fill me in ASAP, buddy. Looks like we have primo space for your article. Front page, too. Seems like fake psychics are hot property! Dude, you really nailed this one, big time! Keep it up buddy. Later."

Silence.

Connor sat and looked at Keighley's house filling the darkness. Suppressing the guilt rising in his throat, like bitter bile, Connor swallowed hard.

A light went on in an upstairs window, glowing through thin amber curtains. Connor longed to join her in that upstairs room, behind that mysterious window, and talk deep into the night. Reluctantly, he started his engine and slowly began the lonely drive home.

Chapter 8

The Clam Basket diner was just winding down from the crowded breakfast rush. Each time the door opened, the small bell pealed and a rush of chilled, salt water air mixed with the homey scent of strong coffee and toasted bread. Late morning light was streaming through the diner's windows and Keighley was sitting at the breakfast bar, dividing up the tip jar. She had worked at the Clam Basket off and on for years and the breakfast crowd, surprisingly, always tipped the best. She shared shifts with another waitress, Janice, who had worked there for over forty years. Janice was a robust woman in her sixties, widowed, and was known for three things: her poker, her cigarettes, and her heart.

"Adam and Eve on a raft!" Janice shouted through the window into the kitchen. "Float 'em!" And with a bang of the small bell, the last breakfast order was placed. She poured Keighley a cup of coffee.

"How'd we do, doll?" she asked, elbows on the counter, chin firmly in her hands, a few grey hairs poking through her hair net.

"Pretty darn good for a weekday rush," Keighley said. "There's about seventy bucks each." Delighted, Keighley thought about a nice a dinner out, a movie, a date, Connor. But it seemed too soon to ask. Besides, it would conflict with his article, so she firmly brushed the thought away.

Janice noticed Keighley looked more tired than usual. "Kiddo, how's your grandpa holding up?" she asked.

"Oh, he's fine. Just fine," Keighley responded, taking a sip of the dark and bitter coffee. "He had a minor fall last night, but it's okay. Just a bruise."

Concerned, Janice looked at her. "Honey," she said, but Keighley wouldn't let her finish.

"It was nothing, really. He's fine. He was just reaching for the remote and slipped out of bed. Bruised up his arm a bit, but I got ice on it right away," she explained.

Janice held on to her concern. "Okay," she said, unsure how to continue. A little more pointedly she added, "And how about you? How are you holdin' up?"

"Janice, I'm fine, really! He's okay. He joked about it a bit too."

"Not what I asked darlin'," Janice responded. She poured herself another cup of coffee and waited patiently for Keighley to spill the beans. "How are you doing in that big old house?"

Keighley knew that when Janice sat with a second cup of coffee, it was talk time. She took a deep breath and spoke to her friend.

"It's fine, really. We could use some repairs, but what house in this ol' town doesn't? Wallpaper could use some work. That damp sea air seems to infect everything, this winter especially! But," she paused, "it does get lonely in there sometimes." She thought a moment. "Janice, sometimes I get so scared. He's a big guy. What happens if he falls and I can't lift him up? Who do I call?"

"That's what 911 is for! Plus you have my number. Use it. And the guys next door, Gary and Jonathan, they'd come running. They love Albert," Janice encouraged.

"I know, I know. It's just, since the stroke, I want to make sure he's home. That I'm the one caring for him, not some stranger in a hospital."

"In this town?" Janice laughed. "Honey, there are no strangers in Cobweb Corners. Everyone in town knows Albert. He'd be surrounded by friends no matter where he is, and he's a hell of a lot stronger than you recognize."

"I know, I know," she said. Though small town living can have its drawbacks—nosy neighbors, small-town gossip and the like. One thing was for sure. People were always there when they were needed. Keighley was thankful for that.

"We had a talk last night, after he fell?" she said, a little tentative about the subject. "He told me about his will and all, again. Years ago he told me the house was paid off and it'll be mine, so no big surprise there. But, ya know? He kept saying the oddest thing. He kept asking if I found the pennies. Over and over, did I find the pennies, did I find the nickels, did I find the dimes. It's weird."

"Pennies?" Janice asked. "You mean that penny jar in the hall?"

"Yeah, and I tell him every time, Pop-Pop, yes, the pennies are in the jar, just where you put them. I try to remind him. Last night? I even took him into the hall and we both looked at, talked about all of his pennies in there, but it gets frustrating, ya know? The same question, fifty times a day." She took a sip of her coffee and thought. "But lately, Janice? He's been getting really obsessed over those pennies."

The kitchen bell rang and Janice got up to serve the final breakfast order.

Keighley held her coffee cup under her lips and saw her reflection in the dark brew. Unlike the crystal ball, her face was reflected back to her with no special mystery, no dramatic flair. Just Keighley, simple and ordinary. She noticed the concerned look around her eyes, the slightly tired expression. She blew on the coffee and her face rolled into a thousand ripples and disappeared into the rising steam.

"Honey, I saw that. Where the devil you just go?" Janice had returned and brought her mom voice with her.

"Well, I wasn't going to say anything," Keighley smiled, "but this guy came by the other day for a reading."

Janice sat. She loved to hear Keighley's stories, though Keighley was far more respectful of her clients' privacy than Janice would be. Janice wanted to hear all the melodramatic details of betrayed lovers and jealous spouses.

"Oh yeah?" Janice asked, pouring herself another cup of coffee.

"Yeah. Young guy, too. Late twenties or so, and cute? Mmm." Both women laughed. Janice noticed the extra sparkle in Keighley's eyes.

"He seemed pretty open to the reading too. Easygoing, ya know? At first he seemed little nervous. A little twitchy. But as we talked and I told him what I do, he eased up. The reading was going great and I could tell he was interested. And his eyes? Brown as a buck's! Mmm!" She laughed. "Anyway, when I got to his heart line and told him want I saw, he got all tensed up, like I hit a nerve or something."

"Maybe you did. Honey," Janice offered, "you know as well as anyone, there are things some people just keep to themselves. Maybe you brought up something he didn't want to discuss."

"I'll say. From that point on, he just shut right down. Wouldn't even stay for the tea. It was weird."

"Honey, nuthin' weird there. He's a young guy! They don't want to talk about those things. Especially with a pretty gal like you. 'Course he took off like a crab on the shore!"

"Yeah, but that's not all." Keighley's voice indicated much more was on the way. "Later that night he called me and guess what?" Keighley paused a moment and took a sip of coffee, keeping Janice entranced. She loved the excitement in Janice's eyes when a good story was going. "Turns out, he's a reporter and he's writing an article on psychics."

"But you're not psychic, so why'd he call you?" Janice asked.

"Who knows? I guess he just lumps us all together like everyone else. An intuitive and a psychic are all the same to these people. He sees a palm reader and just assumes I'm psychic, I guess. I explained what I do as best I could. Told him I don't predict the future. Told him I'm more like a life coach. Funny though. He seemed more interested in the palm reading than the life coaching"

"So?" Janice asked, wanting to know more. "What did you tell him? More importantly—" She leaned forward conspiratorially. "What did he look like again?"

"Janice," Keighley said, leaning back in her seat, "This guy was so fine, he could work in the sewers and I'd still invite him over for dinner. And those arms? His T-shirt looked ready to bust!" The two women laughed heartily. Through the years, they had bonded over their shared isolation. Janice's husband passed away three years ago from a massive heart attack and she had recently discovered that she was still a little randy. She loved these flirtatious stories and hungered for her own.

"So?" she asked. "Tell me more."

"Well, turns out he wasn't there for a reading at all. He's writing an article on fortune tellers for that magazine, *The Road Less Traveled*? You ever see it?"

"Yeah. I've seen it. All those kooks?"

Keighley laughed. "That's the one!" she said. "Anyway, he asked if he could interview me, so he came back the next day for the interview. But Janice, here's the weird thing. This guy seems sincere. He's the real deal, ya know? We sat in the tea garden and talked for a while. He's a nice guy. A little shy, and kind. But … "

"But what?" Janice wanted to know.

"There's something there that I can't quite put my finger on. Something that is just a little off. He's got baggage from his past. It's all over his palm. It's in his eyes too, but hell, we all do. Maybe that's it." She leaned back and thought for a moment. "He was real kind with Pop-Pop, I can tell you that much. Patient and acted like a real gentleman. It was nice to see." She let the image drop. "So, he's coming back for the second interview next week. Who knows. It may drum up more business for me. Lord knows I could use the extra cash."

"Honey, take a couple of shifts here! You know we need the help."

"Can't," she replied. "I don't like to leave Pop-Pop that long. You know how it is. Working out of the house is easier for me right now."

Janice sighed. "Honey, when you gonna go back to school? Your grandpa will be fine. He's stronger than you know. I'll check in on him, the guys next door would. Hell, we all can! You were doing so well in those classes."

And it was true. A few years back, she was accepted on scholarship to the New England Institute of Fine Arts where she studied graphic design and illustration. She was just completing her third year when her grandfather suffered his stroke. Her priorities were strong and Keighley took a leave from the school in order to care for him.

Keighley truly missed her art classes. She had a well-stocked painting studio at the house, thanks to her grandfather, but what she missed most was being around so many young people. At twenty-six, Keighley had a few dates, a not-so-steady boyfriend here and there, but that was all years ago. The memory of her time between the sheets wrapped up in the arms of a strong young guy was fading quickly.

"One day I'll go back. It's just not the right time, ya know? Maybe I can get this guy to model for me!" Both women laughed, but the idea wasn't far from the truth. Keighley needed a new model for her paintings. Pop-Pop was great. He was still, but she hungered for a challenge, and the idea of a naked guy in her studio, this naked guy, warmed her immensely.

She looked deeply into her coffee cup, looking for a sign, and in the dark brew, the face of a smiling women looked back.

Chapter 9

"So, what's up with all the naked people?" Connor asked, a healthy smile glowing across his face.

"They're not naked. They're nudes." Keighley stressed the final word with a slight laugh as she elbowed his ribs. Connor jumped, welcoming the contact. Though done in jest, her arm sent a thousand waves of electric current through his core. He became aware of her presence, her light, her voice, and he wished he could look at her as deeply as they were looking at the paintings.

They were standing in the wide hallway looking at a wall covered in paintings. There must have been over twenty pieces hung in no particular order other than arranged chaos. Small landscapes in bright golden frames hung above large panels of riotously colored nudes while seascapes of unrelenting energy contradicted the solitary interior of the hallway.

The penny jar sat heavily behind them, impatient to be noticed.

Connor stared, entranced by the varying styles and moods of each painting. "So," he asked, "which ones are yours?"

"You tell me," she responded flirtatiously.

He happily accepted the challenge and began to slowly pace the hallway, looking at each unique piece.

Smiling, she watched Connor study the busy wall. Something about being close to this man awakened her quiet spirit. Her body buzzed like a hive of a million bees waiting for the spring thaw. She anticipated the air around his chest, his torso, his thighs, the way a mother bear senses her cubs, and she smiled at the thought. She even dared a glance at his bottom as he studied the paintings. Even under his Levi's it appeared muscular and firm, and she briefly wondered what it would look like without the jeans. Too embarrassed to continue the thought, she broke away and shouted gently down the hall.

"Pop-Pop," she said, "Connor is here for another interview. Will you come out and say hi?" He had been more agitated than usual, and Keighley was concerned.

"I'm fine, I'm fine," he responded over the soft noise of the TV. He sounded a little wheezy, but still robust for a man his age.

"Okay, so far, this one is yours." Connor's voice brought her back. He was pointing to a small interior scene. Encased in a simple oaken frame, a single lamp burned softly on a table against a wall. Next to it a half-opened door revealed a softly lit room. The entire scene was lit with a gentle greenish glow, and though no people were in it, it gave the viewer the contradictory impressions of contentment and loneliness.

"It's really great," he said.

"Thanks!" Keighley responded. "But that's one of my grandfather's. Try again." She laughed, happily challenging him. She was enjoying this game.

He held her eyes and smiled. Was he searching for a clue, a sign for which painting to choose? Or was he hoping for a key? He longed for a sign of interest from her.

He moved to a large painting Keighley did for her advanced figure painting class. It was her final project and brought serious recognition to her abilities. The painting was almost five feet tall and about four feet wide. It hung just off center of the hall and was surrounded in a heavy oak frame.

Wild swirls of reds, pinks, and velvety purples lit a scene of three stylized figures. They were women, dancing in what appeared to be a field of grass. Purple grass. Or maybe it was water? The ocean? They were nude, and their arms alternately stretched toward each other as they appeared to be dancing with the moon, meanwhile a dozen stars pin-pricked the heavens above them. What were they celebrating? It was mysterious and out of reach, yet confident and tangible all at the same time. It was a joyous painting and made everyone who saw it envious of those dancing women.

Connor looked at Keighley. He knew he was falling for this woman—hard.

"Okay, how about this one?" he asked, nodding at the painting.

Keighley smiled at Connor's choice. "Right on the nose, cowboy," she said, then immediately cringed. *Cowboy? Please tell me I did not just say cowboy!*

"Wow. That's pretty wild," Connor replied. Slightly embarrassed by the nudes, he was still intrigued by Keighley's interpretation.

"I did it a few years ago in college. It won a nice scholarship for my senior year, too," she revealed, slightly timid to talk about her past success.

"So I guess these other naked paintings are yours, too?" he asked.

"Not all of them. My grandfather was a really amazing painter in his day. Here, look at this one." She took him by the hand and led him down the hall to the last painting. At the touch of her hand, his brain short-circuited. He decided he'd follow this woman anywhere. If she led him bare-foot over hot coals, he'd follow. As long as her soft hand remained in his muscular paw, his past sorrows seemed to recede into a distant memory, healed, tender, and remote.

They stopped just before the deep hall entered into another room toward the back of the house.

"Pop-Pop," Keighley called. "I'm showing Mr. Jakes your painting of grandma."

"Is that right?" he called back. "It's a nice one of her. I got her eyes right for the first time in that one."

"Connor, I'd like you to meet my grandmother, Hattie Woodson." Keighley smiled at the eccentric introduction, and Connor met the departed Hattie, in the nude.

Hattie was a robust woman, about fifty-five. She was reclining nude on a large white bed, book in one hand, the other arm tossed lazily above her head. But she wasn't reading. She was looking into the viewer's eyes with a coy surprise. Those eyes said volumes. They told the viewer not much reading would be accomplished that afternoon and they invited the viewer, the painter in this case, into the large bed, and into her supple folds and secret recesses. It was voluptuous and honest, real and sincere.

It made some viewers blush.

Of all of the art in their home, Keighley loved this painting the best.

They heard an old voice behind them. "That was my girl, my crazy Hattie," he cooed softly. He walked slowly toward the painting and touched Hattie's painted cheek for a moment.

Keighley stood behind her grandfather. Moved by the love he still felt for his departed wife, Keighley put her arms around this old man. She hugged and kissed his cheek from behind him and looking at this unique family portrait, was moved by the love that resounded in her remaining family.

"It's a beautiful painting, Pop-Pop," she said. "Anyone can see now much you loved her."

Connor felt like he should say something, but how do you compliment another man's naked wife? He decided it was best to say nothing. Awkwardly, he shuffled to the side a bit and let Keighley and her grandfather share this moment. He watched, isolated, yet grateful to be in its glow.

"Young man?" Albert asked. He noticed Connor inching away. "Come over here and look at my wife. She was a beauty."

Keighley noticed Connor was a little uncomfortable and giggled. "Yeah, Connor, come look closely. What do you think?" she teased.

Connor shook his head slightly and approached the sly, smiling pair. They knew exactly what they were doing and he decided to go along with them.

"Well, Sir," he began, respectfully. "Keighley's right. It's a beautiful painting. Anyone can see that."

So far so good.

The smiling couple waited, and with his heart in his throat, Keighley winked at him from over her grandfather's shoulder.

Oh the devil, he thought, loving the challenge.

He continued, slowly. "She looks really content. No. Really sure. Something like that. She, her attitude, it's complete or something." The words weren't coming. Keighley's wink made sure of that.

He paused a moment more.

He considered.

He stepped directly in front of the painting and took another deep breath. Searching his brain for the right words, he started again. "She's glowing," he suddenly acknowledged. "She's looking right at me and she knows something, something I want, something I'm missing." Where these words actually coming from him? "She's comforting, too. She wants to comfort me, us, I mean—whoever is there. That's what it is."

He looked directly at Keighley.

His eyes were shining.

"She's hope,'" he said.

Keighley's smile illuminated the room.

Chapter 10

Keighley's heart began to race. She couldn't believe the words she was hearing. She looked deeply at Connor. The look in his eyes reveled his surprise at his own words, his discovery of the painting's mystery, and perhaps something deeper. He was so handsome, so devastatingly beautiful at that moment, that Keighley fell, right then and there, grateful to land in this man's strong arms.

Pop-Pop noticed too. He was happy to have set this into motion, aided by his late wife. As he walked back to the living room beyond the hall, his job was well completed. He said quietly over his shoulder, "It's all that really matters you know. Comfort from the world, and ..." He seemed to lose the thought. "And ... " he stopped, turned and looked at his granddaughter, hoping she'd supply the missing thought.

"And what, Pop-Pop?" she asked gently.

His eyes darkened a bit as he thought. He spied the penny jar and asked, "Those nickels, where are they?" He looked at her, confused. "I put all those quarters there. Dimes, coins, quarters, silver dollars," he said, suddenly worried. "Did you get them?" He was becoming more confused and agitated. "Where are they? Who took them!" he demanded. He was shaking. The quiet gentleman from a few moments ago was replaced by a bruised, irate soldier battling a forgotten war.

Connor saw the concern in Keighley's eyes and stepped forward. "Sir," he said kindly, "They're right here." He took Albert by the hand and gently guided him to the large penny jar. "Keighley showed them to me last week. See? She told me how you added your pennies to the jar." Connor gently placed

Albert's hand on the large, heavy jar whose presence seemed to weigh more than the world itself at this moment.

Albert looked between this young man and his granddaughter, searching their eyes for truth, for recognition. He knew something was missing, something was wrong, but he couldn't find the words. They were lost in the greyness of his mind, bruised from the stroke, waiting for light that would not return.

Upon touching the cool jug, Albert calmed a bit. He relaxed a little and the moment passed.

"That's it. That's right," he mumbled softly. He looked tired and Keighley stepped forward to help him.

"Pop-Pop," she said. "How about I take you to your room. You can rest a bit before dinner? How does that sound?"

"Good, daughter, that would be good," he replied, mistily.

Keighley gave Connor an I'll-be-right-back look and helped her grandfather shuffle down the hall.

Connor watched entranced as they disappeared. He heard Keighley's soft voice as she aided her grandfather. A few mumbled replies from a raspy throat.

He never experienced this kind of love. Not with his own parents, not with Randy even. He sat on the dark hallway bench and tried to push the memory of Randy aside, but she didn't always like to stay put. He sighed heavily and wondered what new life he was heading for.

⊗

Keighley returned and stood on the dim part of the hall watching Connor. He was so warm, so inviting as he sat there lost in thought. The setting sun wove honeyed light through the curtained window in the front door and cast this man in a familiar amber glow. Who was he? Where did he come from? He put his face in his hands like he was trying to recover from something unpleasant. She longed to find the route into his mystery and heal whatever pain he was remembering.

"You're a kind man, Connor Jakes," she said, speaking from the dimness just beyond his reach.

He looked up at her, thankful for her return.

"Thank you for helping my grandpa. That was really nice of you," she said.

"Sure, yeah. No problem," he replied. "How's he doing?"

"He'll be okay," she said. "Sometimes, he gets a little confused, and lately, he's been obsessing over the coin jar. It's weird. He's resting now." She paused a moment. "We should probably go on the porch so we don't disturb him."

"Actually," he responded, whispering lowly, "I'd really like to see more of your paintings. Do you have more down here?"

She smiled at him, and whispered, "I can do better than that. Come upstairs and I'll show you my studio." She was grinning like the Cheshire cat.

She took his hand and led him upstairs.

Chapter 11

Her heart beat wildly with anticipation. Everything with this man seemed so natural, so elemental, that when she took his hand in hers, it felt like it had always been there, through all of the seasons, invisible and unseen, yet always present and sure.

The wide oak staircase reached up into the darkness. Its familiar creaks and groans seemed to protest more loudly under the unfamiliar weight of this solid man, yet each step the young couple took encouraged the familiar tread to accept the burden and, indeed, welcome it.

Like everything in this house, the staircase was a marvel of design, yet left unfettered, it lost its radiance and sunk into the territory of the ignored and overlooked. Ten steps led up to a landing, a sharp turn to the left, and about five more revealed the second floor. The wide oak banister was smooth from offering nearly two centuries of safety to small unsteady hands. Tonight it welcomed Keighley's soft palm, stroking its surface, grazing its dusty plane so the memory of her finger tips remained like snail trails across a dry smooth stone.

Connor followed closely behind.

When they reached the top, Keighley warned politely, "The hallway light died years ago. Just follow me."

She led Connor through a fun-house maze of thin hallways haunted with aged wallpaper in peeling arabesques, remnants from previous centuries. They walked around corners, side stepped a book case with bursting shelves stuffed with dry and brittle bindings. Feeble light from a curtained window at the end of a hall revealed a myriad of tightly closed doors along the route. The hallway was a wonderland of shadows and tightly closed doors where at any moment, a goblin, a ghoul, a crazed clown could spring out and snatch away the unwary traveler.

One more corner and, "Here we are," she said, pausing in front of her studio room door. She was nervous. It had been years since anyone, even Pop-Pop, had been inside her studio. And now? Not only was she about to reveal this private space of her creative spirit, but she was about to reveal it to him, this guy, Connor. Her heart beat rapidly, like butterfly wings at dawn.

She opened the door and stepped aside.

It was nothing like Connor had imagined. It was nothing like Connor had ever seen.

It was everything Connor had hoped it would be.

He stepped inside.

It was a large room, perhaps the largest in the house. He noticed that it was also the lightest room as well. It didn't have the antique weight that sagged the other rooms in this mysterious home. It was missing the burden of history that seemed to permeate every wall.

Instead, this tall-ceilinged room was filled with light, air and serenity.

Keighley smiled as she watched Connor enter her room.

The warm scent of oil paint hung in the air like a memory of morning fog. All around him were the signs of a productive and creative artist. Two large easels leaned against the wall while another stood about ten feet from him, centering the room by its magnetic presence. Canvases of unframed paintings lined the walls: unashamed nudes and loose landscapes, interiors and abstracts, while a hundred small illustrations tacked to a cork board fluttered enviably for his recognition.

Keighley watched as Connor absorbed her space. She was relieved he was so quiet as he walked through her studio. His eyes slowly swept over each space, the old fireplace against the wall to his left, the studio couch lost under a hundred pillows and throws, counter tops loaded with silvery wrinkled paint tubes the size of fat, curled fingers, tin cans bursting with a thousand brushes—all of it received his thoughtful gaze.

Though the room was abundantly filled, it never appeared

crowded or messy.

It was comfortable.

It was inviting.

It was home.

He walked forward and gazed at the far wall. It was a huge window, over ten feet long and just about as high. It seemed alive as its thin, gauzy curtain, the color of buttery custard, danced lazily from the slight ocean breeze.

Keighley stepped forward to shut the window. "I was painting this morning," she said. "I love to let the morning air in. Especially when I'm working."

"What are you working on?" he asked, hoping to surrender to the sound of her voice.

"Take a look," she offered and pointed to the easel in the center of the room. Its back was to them, and she watched Connor circle to its front.

"I started it last month," she explained. "I was watching Pop-Pop in the garden. He sat in the lavender and Ginger jumped in his lap. I grabbed a brush and just started painting."

"Wow," he said, once again searching for words. Why was language so foreign when he was close to her? "It's going to be amazing."

It was a beautiful painting. Keighley wanted to put all of the love she felt for this old man into the colors and texture of his body, his person, his soul. And she captured it too. Perhaps it was the gentle landscape, perhaps it was in the simple way his withered hand stroked Ginger the cat, or perhaps in was in the simple grace of his expression that captivated a life well lived.

She suddenly noticed Connor's stillness beside her. She longed to lean into him. To feel his strong arms wrap around her. She wanted to turn to him and bury her face in his solid neck, to breathe in his warm, earthy scent of salt and grass. To taste the skin grazing his square jaw. It would taste like pine and smoked whiskey. She knew it.

It had been far too long since she allowed a guy into her life and she hungered for Connor's strength. His firm chest, his smooth stomach, his strong thighs. Suddenly embarrassed by the tension filling them both, she smiled and took a slight step away.

"I'm glad you like it," she said. "I haven't shown it to Pop-Pop yet. I'm saving it for Christmas."

Connor sighed. Standing next to her was more than he could bear. He was on fire, burning from within. His thighs were charged with a hundred volts while a thousand hornets winged their way through his veins, alive for the first time in years.

"Oh," he responded, attempting to sound calm, hoping to master his nervous voice. "That's nice."

They were both silent for a moment, neither one was aware how to proceed, both relishing the glow of their shared silent desire.

"Connor, I want to ask you something." Keighley broke the silence.

"Sure, what is it?" he asked, knowing full well that if she asked him to eat rusty nails at this moment, he'd do so, happily employed by her smile.

"Since I've been out of art school, it's been hard to get live models," she smiled, a little embarrassed to proceed.

Connor raised one brown eyebrow, curious to hear the rest yet nervous about its result.

"Yeahhh," he said anxiously, a half-smile turning his mouth.

"Well, I want to do more life studies, and to do that I need real models. I can't do a dozen paintings of Pop-Pop. So—" She lingered on the question. "I figured, since I'm helping you with your article, you could help me with a painting or two?"

Her slightly raised eyebrow indicated he wouldn't need a pressed shirt or clean slacks for this job.

Connor blushed, embarrassed by the sudden tightness growing in his jeans.

"Um, me?" was the best he could manage.

She laughed. "Yes, you!" she said. "You've got good light around you. I'd like to try to work it into a painting or two, ya know?" She stepped closer to him and the electricity grew stronger, warmer, as she hoped it would. "And don't worry, you can use a sheet if you're scared." She teasingly tapped a finger on his solid chest, letting it rest there a moment longer, building the fire passing between them.

Connor knew what was coming. He was silent. He was nervous. He was ablaze with desire. He looked at Keighley, and from under his brown eyes full of devotion, he whispered softly, "Keighley, I think I want to kiss you." He dared. He paused. "But I'm not … sure how."

Oh my God, she thought, loving the simple honestly in this guy.

She paused a moment and let his simple request hang in the charged air around them.

"Like this," she said. Her smile lit up the room like starlight and radiated through his wounded heart.

She held his hand softly at his side and reached up to kiss him. She didn't meet his lips right away. Instead, she paused just a breath away and enjoyed the electricity radiating between their lips before she took her first sweet taste. She breathed in his muscular scent, deeply, anticipating the craving that consumed them both. She leaned into him and melted as she felt his solid heart beating through his tight T-shirt, like a strong bird under a cotton sheet, silently thudding against her breasts.

It filled her.

Her heart raced. She prolonged the first kiss moment a second more, loving the way his strong chest, his solid muscles felt against her languid body. He took a quick, sharp breath and waited, allowing her to control the movement, the pace, and the temperature.

And she did, expertly.

Standing on tiptoe, she leaned in. Their lips met in a whisper. It was supple and strong and she sighed as she let him in. Slowly, she traced his lips with her tongue. They tasted of earth and copper, of crushed leaves and autumnal sea air.

Her yearning, which had slept comfortably for years, was now wide awake and ready to fulfill its promise. She realized it was good.

It was needed.

It was Connor. She found her home and welcomed its return.

ೞ

The crash in the hallway shook them from their private world. Like a hundred windows shattering in a storm of stones, the house shook from this unnatural cry.

A muffled shout, another loud crash and "Pop-Pop!" Keighley shouted. She bolted from Connor's arms and was out the door in seconds. Connor followed close behind.

They flew down the hall, around the corner and there stood Pop-Pop, like a wolf tearing at the bars of a cage. Streams of shredded wallpaper surrounded his feet while a few strands remained on the wall like brittle, dry leaves bracing against the cruel winter wind.

Books littered the floor like an exploded library while the confused man moaned, "Where are they? Who took them?" He looked at Keighley and shouted, "Someone stole your money. I left it right here. It was for you!" he cried. "All my quarters. All my gold! It's gone!" He attacked the wall again.

"Pop-Pop! Stop! Please, stop!" she begged. "I have it. You gave it to me? Remember? It's in the jug." She tried to calm him. She began to walk over the debris of shattered books and slashed wallpaper, and that's when she noticed the blood.

"Oh my God. Connor, help me." Her voice was shaking.

Albert's arm was covered in blood. "Pop-Pop," she said, trying to sound calm, "you cut yourself. We need to help you? Okay? Just stay there." She looked frantically at Connor.

Connor moved gently toward the frightened man who was too confused to notice his condition. "Sir," he asked. "How about letting me take a look at that arm?" he requested as he moved slowly toward Albert.

When he reached the old man, he gently said over his shoulder, "Keighley, call 911, now." Keighley frantically dialed her cell, and quickly gave instructions, begging them to hurry.

Slowly, Connor sat Albert on the floor amidst the littered books, "Have a seat, Sir," he said calmly. "Let me see about that cut, okay?" Connor saw it was more than a cut. It was a deep gash that continuously pumped blood down the old man's arm. Connor saw the shattered mirror next to them.

Their reflections exploded in ruby tinted fragments.

"You'll be just fine, Sir," he said. He quickly removed his T-shirt, wrapped it around Albert's bleeding arm and pressed on the large gash with both of his strong hands.

He looked up at Keighley, hoping his eyes didn't betray the gravity of the situation while warm blood soaked through his fingertips.

Chapter 12

The starch enameled walls of the emergency room burned Keighley's eyes as she waited to hear. Bright fluorescent lights above lit them both in an unnatural icy glow. Connor sat next to her, holding her hand, reaffirming what he knew. Pop-Pop would be okay.

A young doctor entered the waiting room. She looked vaguely familiar, and approached the concerned pair.

"Keighley Woodson? I'm Dr. Leslie Clements. I just tended to your grandfather."

"How is he? Is he okay?" Keighley's concern tumbled from her mouth.

Connor stood beside her. His hand never left her side.

"He's fine. He'll be fine," she reassured Keighley. "He has quite a deep cut. We cleaned it and stitched it up. He'll be just fine. He's resting now."

"Oh thank God," Keighley sighed in great relief, the tears began to fall again. With a small gesture, Dr. Clements invited Keighley to sit. Connor stood nearby, patiently waiting to see if he was needed.

"He's got eight stitches below the left elbow. He'll heal up in no time, but there'll be quite a scar." Dr. Clements paused a moment. "When he first arrived, he seemed quite confused. Can you tell me what happened?"

Keighley's eyes grew large. "I don't know. I don't know!"

Her head was spinning. She didn't know where to start. The tears were flowing freely, yet she never allowed them to distort her concern into chaos. She took a breath and tried to begin. "We were in the studio and heard a crash. I thought it was my cat, but then we heard his voice. He was yelling and he … " Keighley didn't know how to continue. Did she say she was distracted, kissing a guy, fooling around, and forgot where Pop-Pop was? She refused to express what she had feared most of all: that Pop-Pop was becoming more and more ungrounded and she was not prepared for the shift.

Connor stepped forward. "Dr. Clements," he said. "It seems that Albert was confused about where he put some cash. He keeps it in a jar on the first floor. He was on the second floor and I guess he became confused for a moment. When we found him, he was bleeding from a broken mirror. That's when we called 911."

The doctor looked at Keighley. "Does he get confused often?" she asked gently. She saw Keighley's fear and proceeded softly.

Keighley held the doctor's eyes for a moment, searching for trust. "Since his stroke, yes, a little," she said. Then, more firmly, "Yes, he has. It's been—" She paused and collected her thoughts. Connor stood by, prepared to help if needed. "Since his stroke, he's had a few spells where he forget things and he gets a little confused, but never like this."

"A man with his history? I'm not surprised," the doctor reassured. "Of course he gets confused now and then. However, I'm concerned about his safety. Has he been violent before this episode?"

"No! Never! Really, this was the first time I've seen him like this, really!" Keighley began to panic. She didn't like where the conversation was headed.

"Keighley, it's okay," Dr. Clements said smoothly. "Nothing is going to happen. I just want to make sure he'll be okay when we release him. That you'll both be okay."

"Release him? What? What do you mean?"

"We had to give him a sedative. He's sleeping pretty soundly right now. Orbiting Jupiter hopefully," she smiled and looked compassionately at Keighley. "That's a good thing. Sleep heals the body in wonderful ways. He'll sleep through the night. We'll check him over in the morning, and you can take him home before lunch."

Keighley sighed in relief and looked at Connor. His eyes

were shining and he smiled softy at Keighley.

Dr. Clements interrupted the moment. She looked at Keighley and said, "You look like you could use some sleep yourself. How are you holding up?"

For the first time all night, Keighley felt like she was finally able to breathe. "I'll be okay," she said. Relieved that Pop-Pop would be okay and comforted by Connor's warm presence, Keighley turned to go.

"By the way," the doctor called. "I'll see you at the diner soon, okay? You guys make the best feta omelets in New Hampshire!" She smiled brightly at Keighley.

Keighley turned to her, finally placing her face in her memory. Dr. Clements was a regular at the Clam Basket Diner. She must have waited on her a dozen times.

Keighley smiled. "That'd be great," she said smiling in recognition, "and your next omelet is on me."

Keighley and Connor stepped outside the emergency doors into a crisp darkness. It was past two in the morning. The silence and the night air was as refreshing as a cool cotton sheets on a hot summer night. Keighley stopped for a moment and looked up into the vast night sky. She listened to the waves pounding in the distance and took in a deep breath of cleansing air. She held it in her lungs, thankful for the doctor's words, for Connor's attention, for Pop-Pop's life.

A gift to her spirit.

Connor watched her. She seemed at perfect peace as she looked into that deep sky and held it in her lungs, her hair gently waving in the crisp night breeze.

He felt abundance, and most of all, gratitude.

What is it about her?

Chapter 13

When Connor pulled into the driveway of 1111 Pynchon Farm Road, the darkness enveloped the yard. Keighley was sound asleep next to him, her head softly resting on his shoulder.

The gravel driveway gently crunched under the wheels as he slowly pulled the car to a stop, killed the headlights, and turned off the engine.

Silence.

A cricket.

A lonesome bird call from above.

He sat still, staring into the dark ahead and loving this moment. Keighley safely asleep on his shoulder. The whole world still and silent. If he could, he would package this feeling to open whenever he needed it—in his lonely home when memories of Randy hurt his core, his holidays alone.

This moment was enough to live off of, he realized with a smile. This intriguing woman, her loving grandfather, her crazy house. Her vibrant spirit. He knew he was falling in love, and he welcomed it like a long-waited for guest, arriving without warning. But this time was different. This time, it felt more … real? *No, that's not it,* he thought. *True? No, that's not it either.* Something natural, something that springs from the earth as it should, and grow as it is supposed to. That doesn't get cut down. Something that lasts effortlessly.

Elemental.

That was it.

Yes, he thought as a smile crept across his firm jaw.

Keighley stirred on the seat beside him. She lifted her head a bit and blinked slowly. "Where are we?" she asked sleepily.

"We're home, babe," he said, then gulped. Babe, he said.

Did she hear? Did she notice? It just fell into place without thought or reason, simple as the night air.

And at that moment, Connor chose to follow this path that led him to this beautiful palm reader. Did she even know how beautiful she was he wondered?

"I'll get the door for you," he said. He ran to her side of the car, opened the door, and helped the sleepy woman into the night air. She stood a little unsteadily, wobbled a bit as she tried to catch her balance. She laughed slightly, then before she knew it, she was weightless, curled up in the arms of this strong man who was carrying her to her house. She put both of her arms around his neck and relaxed. Melted really. Their bodies fit like two puzzle pieces that had been reunited after a long journey.

She rested her chin upon his muscular shoulder and for a moment, wished she could sleep there, safe, surrounded, resting against his flannel shirt and breathing in the rich scent of the earth that rose from his musky chest. *If I could,* she thought, *I'd bottle up this moment and keep it—forever.*

They tackled the porch steps and stopped in front of the door. Ginger was curled up in the wicker chair awaiting their arrival. She meowed and jumped down, happy for their return.

"Hey girl," she said with care, reluctant to leave this man's embrace. Being held above the earth, crunched up in the strong arms of this compassionate guy was better than a dream. She gave him one last squeeze, just so he'd notice and said whispered sleepily into his ear, "Connor, my keys are stabbing into my hip!"

He laughed, heartily, and set her down. Ginger curled around her legs, impatient to get inside. Next to the door, she noticed two jars of canned peaches on the floor. Topped with red gingham squares, a small note read, *Albert, enjoy with breakfast, love, Ruth Sylvane.*

That's sweet, Keighley thought. Mrs. Sylvane was always thinking of Pop-Pop.

As she fished in her pocket for the house keys, she looked up at him. "Connor," she said, a little more awake, "thank you. For tonight, I mean. Helping me with … Um." She tried to wrap language and gratitude into a neat package expressing all that occurred over the last ten hours, and couldn't. She realized she didn't want to say good night either. She was fumbling with her keys when she dropped them with a thud.

Connor bent down to retrieve them. He noticed Ginger and gave the cat a gentle scratch, picked up the canned fruit jars, and let them in. Ginger flew through the open door and disappeared.

Keighley stood inside and turned to thank him again, to somehow manage to say goodnight.

"I'm not leaving until you're sound asleep," he said softly shutting the large door behind them. "It's okay, I'll be here," he said reassuringly.

Relief flooded her core. She didn't want to be alone in this old house with too many doors. She had dreaded the day when Pop-Pop would not return, leaving her alone, for good.

"Let me help you," he said. And with that, he swept her up. Once more she was nested against his firm chest and he started up the stairs. Keighley smiled, and nestled her face into his thick neck, thankful for his company, his strength, and his solid arms.

The wide oak staircase welcomed this early morning's burden and embraced the young couple. With strength and gratitude, it guided them to the safe promise of slumber.

"Keighley, close your eyes," he said when he reached the thin hallway. He didn't want Keighley to see the remains of Pop-Pop's battle. She hung on tightly, her face buried in the crook of his neck. She heard his feet brushing past the scattered books, she felt curls of peeled wallpaper brushing against her arm. As he balanced against the uneven path of debris, she heard the crunching broken glass and stiffened against his body.

"It's okay, I got ya," he said as he maneuvered them beyond the painful battlefield.

They arrived at her studio door, and Connor carried her to the large day bed which rested against the window. He set her down amongst the pillows and colorful throws and laid her head on the large feather pillow, which dominated them all.

Ginger followed the pair into the room and curled up on the foot of the bed, purring contentedly.

He covered Keighley with the soft ancient tapestries and velvet throws that littered the studio, until she looked like a pre-Raphaelite princess … Waiting to be kissed.

She smiled.

They looked at each other for a long time.

Eyes locked.

Hearts beating in rhythm.

Measured breath.

Time wonderfully frozen.

The memory of his deep kiss awakened in her. His taste of copper and salt, his scent of hay and earth. She yearned for him to lay next to her, with her, beside her, under a million blankets whose warmth had covered a million lovers before them. How could she tell him? She wanted to sleep with her cheek against his bare chest, nuzzled in the fur that grew across his pecs, her arms around his solid stomach. But tonight?

Confusion reigned.

"Connor," she said lowering her eyes.

"No, don't say anything," he requested gently. "Just sleep." He reached across and brushed the hair away from her face. "I'll take care of everything, okay?" He looked at her a moment longer, amazed by what he discovered in her, then softly leaned down and brushed her forehead with a kiss.

"Go to sleep," he said. "I'll be here."

She curled up a bit and inched toward him. "You're still going to model for me." She laughed gently and reached for his hand. Under a mountain of soft velvet, she slept, the memory of his lips soothing her to sleep.

Connor stayed by her side, thirty minutes? An hour? Two? Time was meaningless as he watched her float into a healing deep slumber, the best of all possible sleeps. Finally, he stood quietly and moved toward the door, trying not to wake the sleeping beauty, hoping against all odds he'd be able to awaken her in the morning with a kiss.

When he reached the hallway, he pulled out his cell phone, hoping its display would add enough light to navigate the impossible hall and saw a missed text from Brian. Ignoring it, he began his task. In the dim, feeble light, he got to his knees and began cleaning up the debris from Albert's episode in the hall. Keighley did not need any reminders of the ordeal, and the easier he could make it for her, the better he felt.

Books were stacked, broken glass was swept, ripped wallpaper was balled and tossed. He inspected the wall that had received Albert's rage. The old man still had a lot of punch in him, that's for sure. Dented by his pounding fists, scarred by torn wallpaper, the wall looked like it was on the losing end of a bad bar fight and had the blood to prove it. One of Albert's fists nearly broke through the wall, too. The blows seemed too deliberate, the dents too deep.

What was he after?

Connor sighed as he finished the chore. He walked down the large staircase, thankful for the silence the old house contained within its walls. He quietly shut the large front door behind him and stood on the front porch for a cleansing breath of air. A weak pink haze crossed the horizon. Sunrise.

He took a deep breath. *What am I doing?* he thought. His strong chest tightened with panic.

I can't be ready for this. I'm not ready for this. I can't. His heart began to beat more rapidly. He recognized what was happening. He allowed himself to care for someone again, too strongly, and she knew it too. He sighed heavily and felt tension rising in his neck.

Oh no. Not now, please not now, he thought. Just when the painful memories of Randy were healing by time, they sprung forward and leapt into his throat. He tensed and tried to suppress the images but they jumped through his mind like wild horses, unable to be tamed, hooves raised, breaking down the doors that kept the memories restrained.

Squeezing his eyes tightly, he forced those doors shut with the will of iron and steel. The horses calmed and retreated behind the heavy doors Connor created to protect himself. He could still hear them pacing around inside, in that pen in the deep corners of his mind, waiting for the next opportunity to bolt, to show themselves, to rage against the light.

He looked at the text from Brian:

Dude, gr8 news! Expanding to a cable show. We need to talk! This psychic quack stuff hot! Meet me Tuesday at Walden's, 1:00. Let's get this baby rolling! Producers meeting in two weeks!

Connor leaned against the old home for support, and swore under his breath.

Chapter 14

The wings were on fire. Smacking his way through the pungent burn, Connor managed to bite all he could from the small bone, tossed it on the plate with a satisfied shrug, and took a long pull from his beer, enjoying the cool burn slide down his throat. He looked at the crimson plate of hot wings in front of him, and dove in again.

"Connor, dude! Slow down man! You're gonna choke." Brian laughed as he waved his empty scotch glass in the air. The ice cubes rattled, signaling the waitress who winked in return.

"Sorry man," Connor replied. "Was a long night and I'm starving. Feel like I haven't eaten in weeks." Connor swiped a napkin across his mouth, tingling from the pungent hot sauce, and took another long pull from his beer. He leaned against the booth's vinyl back and surveyed the pub. Walden's was filled with the typical lunch crowd, a few businessmen and college kids. The air was thick with the scent of brew and hops while tunes were piped through tinny speakers nailed to the dusty beams overhead.

"What'll I get cha, handsome?" The waitress had returned. She eyed Connor while Brian ordered another scotch and water.

"You want another beer?" she asked. "How 'bout a dozen steamers? Just off the boat!"

Connor smiled. "Yeah, that'd be great."

"Comin' right up," she said and headed toward the bar.

Connor's attention returned to Brian. "So, what's this all about? Why the urgent meeting?" He reached for another wing and dove in.

"I've got an offer for you," Brian stated. He leaned forward, demanding Connor's attention. "A cable station has taken some interest in *The Road Less Traveled*." His smile beamed with possibilities. "They've made us a generous offer on it too," he said. "Seems they want to turn it into a weekly program. An hour show, once a week, kind of an evening magazine thing."

"Wow, man, that's awesome." Connor was truly impressed.

"Yeah! I'm floored. Now listen to this. We proposed each episode be divided into four, fifteen-minute segments. We'd use the magazine's name and format, too. Divide the show into chapters, you follow?"

"Yeah, sounds great!" Connor replied. "So what's this got to do with me?" He attacked another wing.

"I suggested you as the host."

Connor stared wide-eyed, chicken wing frozen mid-bite. A quarter sized drop of cherry red sauce plopped from the wing to his shirt, leaving blood red evidence of his stunned silence.

"What? No! No, no, no. No, not me. You're insane. I …" Connor tried wiping his mouth, but the burn didn't subside.

"Now slow down a minute. Connor, you're perfect for this," Brian explained. Trying to build Connor's enthusiasm could be more difficult than he imagined. "Let me explain before you jump the gun. Dude, you're perfect! You've got the whole New England package in your pocket."

"Brian, no way! Not a chance. I can't …" Connor tried to interrupt, but Brian was on a powerful roll.

"Now hold on. Just listen to me," Brian continued. "First, I control the four segments' content, based on our magazine's focus: people, home, history, and the wild card. Get it? The people segment would focus on minor New England celebrities, unusual types, that kind of thing. The home segment would look at unique homes in the region, architecture, gardening blah blah blah."

"Here's your order, fellas. " The waitress returned with her tray of precariously balanced drink orders and served the guys. "Steamers up in a minute. Anything else?"

"No, this is great. Thanks," Brian said, and returned back to Connor without missing a beat. "Entertainment is just that, but like our magazine, we'll be less commercial and more original, ya know? The kooky side-show stuff. Bread and puppet theater, the street artists, that guy with the fence made with bowling balls and old bicycles."

"Yeah, I'm following," Connor replied, a little suspicious as to where he fit in.

"The final segment is called *The Wild Card*," Brian said, with a wide grin.

"And I'm the Joker, right?" Connor was beginning to follow the scope.

"You got it! Each week, you'd introduce a wild topic — haunted lighthouses, graveyard mysteries, urban legends — that kind of thing."

Connor stared, wide-eyed in disbelief.

"We'd start filming in late July, maybe August. So, here's my proposal. We run the fortune teller article earlier than scheduled, say September. That way, we get readers psyched for a series special edition in October. You know, possessed tea sets, ghostly hitch hikers, whacky psychics, that kind of thing. The timing couldn't be better! What do you think?"

Connor was silent for a while. Suddenly the burn from the spicy wings was mild compared to the burn in his reeling brain.

"Brian, man, I'm not a host! I'm a writer, and not a very good one either," he replied, suddenly quite serious.

"Connor, you're the best writer we have!" Brian leaned forward and became more serious. "In fact, you're better than what we need. I've told you that. You know it and I know it. Stop kidding yourself, man. You're good! What happened to that collection of short stories you were working on? Get back to it. Publishers were biting for a look! You have a rare talent. Good writers are born, not made. You, my friend, are a born writer."

"Okay, but I'm not a host, by any means!" Connor responded.

"Hold it a minute. Let me explain." Brian took a quick gulp of his scotch, and dove in, more energetic than before.

"Connor, you've got the charisma, the charm! The chicks will eat it up and the grannie crowd will want to bake you cookies! The guys will dig the whacked out stories and will identify with you. Hell, they'll want to be you!" Brian laughed. "It's perfect man! Look, all you have to do is just look at a camera and talk. Easy as that. We'll take care of the rest."

Connor leaned back and sighed heavily. "This is too much right now," he said.

"What do you mean? Man it's perfect! Perfect! You studied journalism in college! You hosted that campus news show. It'll be like getting back on a horse, I swear," Brian encouraged. "Think of the money too. It's a major—" He leaned forward to stress the point. "—major salary increase."

"I'm fine, Brian. I'm fine," Connor responded. "The insurance settlement saw to that. The house is paid for. I don't even need a job right now."

Brian paused. He understood. He thought for a moment before he proceeded. Not usually one for tact, Brian regrouped his thoughts into a more subtle approach.

"Buddy," he said. "I've watched you. I've seen you every week since Randy—"

"I know! I know," Connor interrupted.

"It's been two years, man. Time to get back on the horse. Time to start living again, ya know? So you don't need money." He paused and held his scotch. He swirled the ice around in his drink, watching it swiftly circle the highball glass, and asked pointedly, "What do you need?" He paused.

His compassion took Connor by surprise.

Connor looked across the table in troubled silence.

"Think about it, okay?" Brian encouraged. "Keep working on the fortune tellers gig, keep the research growing, but we'll put a hold on the article. We'll visit it again this summer as we plan the cable segment and release them together—it's perfect marketing, man. In the meantime, how about digging out those short stories again? Get creative again! Get those juices flowing. It'll be good for you."

Brian was right.

Connor knew it.

He looked across the table and smiled. For the first time in years he felt the drive to create again. He missed writing.

Three years ago, he put away his collection of unfinished

short stories. They weren't jelling. He couldn't connect the dots. Frustrated, he gave up. Then, after the accident, the drive to create died.

Remembering Keighley's request to model for her warmed him. He took a long pull from his beer and smiled. Something was beginning anew.

The spark was returning and tonight, it might ignite in Keighley's studio.

Chapter 15

"Honey! You did what?" Janice nearly choked on her words. Her laugh was loud and robust. She placed a plate with a slice of quiche and salad on the cook's window counter. "Hey Joe!" she yelled into the noisy kitchen. "You see this Reuben? It's supposed to be the fried clam special. So how about waving your magic spatula over the plate and turn it into a plate of clams for me?"

The cook growled a few mumbled words in return, grabbed the sandwich.

"I know, I can't believe it," Keighley replied, giggling into her hands. "I can't believe I got the nerve to ask him!"

"Baby, what I can't believe is that he said yes. That boy is going to pose naked while you paint? You are one lucky lady!" She winked. "Can I get a ticket to that show?"

Keighley laughed again, embarrassed, and loaded up her arms with the final lunch order. "Thanks, Joe. That's it for me." She made her way to the table, arms balancing platters like a tight rope walker.

The lunch crowd was dwindling down at the Clam Basket. A few random tables remained and the chatter had died down to comfortable conversations as patrons finished their coffee and paid their bills. The plates that bustled from the kitchen loaded with sandwiches and chowder, were returned wiped clean with a swipe of buttered French bread.

Keighley stopped by her final remaining table. "Hey Mrs. Sylvane. Is there anything else you want? More coffee?"

"No, honey. I'm fine. Lunch was just wonderful as always." Mrs. Sylvane was a lunch regular and frequently scheduled her palm reading appointments with Keighley when she dined at the cafe.

"Honey, I'll be by Thursday at four, same time as always. Okay with you?"

"Sure thing," Keighley replied cheerfully. "I have a fresh batch of spring mint growing. It's spreading like crazy! It'll make the most wonderful tea. You'll love it. Young mint is so green, it looks like emeralds—tastes like it too!"

Both women laughed gently, then Mrs. Sylvane asked, "Keighley, how's Albert ... your Pop-Pop doing? I was so worried when I heard of his bad spell." Her concern was warm and endearing.

Keighley took a small breath. "Oh he's fine, he's fine. I don't know what came over him. He broke a mirror and got a pretty bad cut, but the doctors cleaned him up and he's on the mend."

"Good. Good, that's a fine thing. Did he get the preserves I left for him?"

"Oh yes, and he's loving them! Thank you. He loads up his breakfast toast with a big spoonful each morning. Opening up that jar is like looking into a big bowl of sunshine he says!"

"Is that so?" Mrs. Sylvane smiled. "Well, he always did have a way with words, didn't he? Must be the artist in him. He always knows how to say just the right thing." Keighley noticed the smile lingering on the kindly woman's face. Her eyes held a momentary youthful smile too.

"Would it be okay if I dropped by this afternoon? Just for a visit of course. Albert is such a nice man."

"I'm sure he'd love that," Keighley replied. She saw Mrs. Sylvane's grin broaden and for a moment, she appeared like a young girl again.

"Wonderful! I'll bring him more of those preserves he likes so much. And a pound cake too. I know he loves my pound cake," she said. "Maybe an afternoon game of canasta? We can ask those nice boys next door to join us. We all used to play canasta years ago. Your grandmother, Hattie, was quite a player in her day. Nobody in town could top her!" She chuckled at the memory and her smile warmed the cafe. "Here's the bill. Keep the change!" and with that, Mrs. Sylvane was out the door and into the warm afternoon. Summer was reaching Cobweb Corners and brought with it fresh Canadian air scented with new possibilities.

Keighley watched Mrs. Sylvane cross the sidewalk. She appeared a woman on a joyful mission and Keighley smiled slightly to herself. She picked up the remaining few plates for the table, a little lost in thought. What was that all about? she wondered as she returned the plates to the kitchen.

"Janice," she said, "Did you hear that?"

"Hear what? Got my last order in and I'm ready for a break."

"Mrs. Sylvane. She was asking about Pop-Pop."

"Sure she was! She likes Albert," Janice responded as she wiped down the cafe's counter.

"No. This was different," Keighley replied, trying to find the words. "Janice, I think Mrs. Sylvane is, well, could she, I mean?" The words weren't forming.

"Honey, where are your eyes?! That lady has had the hots for your grandpa for ages! Where've ya been?"

Keighley's face froze for a moment, then immediately lit up and she laughed aloud. Joyfully. Her laugh reached the air and exploded like notes on a perfectly tuned piano. No wonder! Things were making sense now. The frequent questions, the random deliveries of perfectly preserved jams and jellies, cinnamon buns and pound cakes left by the front door.

"Oh my God," she said, stunned by her inability to have recognized the budding romance. "Why didn't I see this? Really! Really? Where've I been?"

"Honey, you've been so busy trying to keep things together in that big old house, you didn't have any room left over in your head. It's too full," Janice said.

Joe pounded on the order bell. "Yo! Janice! Here's that Reuben that turned into fried clams. Grab it before it turns into a fish cake!"

"That's why I love ya, Joe!" she said. She grabbed her final lunch order. Passing Keighley she whispered, "Looks like you could use a little of the same medicine that Mrs. Sylvane is taking." Then Janice was gone.

Keighley grabbed the tip jar, sat at the counter and begin to divide up the tips, but Janice's words were too distracting, too abundant, too true.

She sighed and stopped counting. She thought of Pop-Pop. She thought of Connor. The memory of his lips still lingered on hers and a dull fear suddenly clutched her heart.

"Honey, I know that look." Janice returned, heaved herself into the chair next to Keighley. "All right, spill the beans."

"It's nothing. It's nothing," Keighley said, but her eyes were telling a different tale.

"Keighley. I know you. I've worked next to you for years and I know what's going on in that head of yours. So talk to me."

"It's just Pop-Pop," she said. "He got so confused, I don't know if I can … The house, it's falling apart and now Mrs. Sylvane and then Connor … What am I doing?"

"You're doing everything just fine. You can't control the world, no matter how hard you try."

"I know, I know. But what do I do about Mrs. Sylvane? How do I …?"

Janice looked at her young friend. The young, she thought, always try to control too much and in the process, life glides by too swiftly. "You let that alone and let those cards fall where they may. It would be good for Albert. It would be great for Mrs. Sylvane. She needs a job. Caring for your grandfather would be perfect for her. Hell, it would be wonderful for you too."

Janice paused a moment before continuing.

"And, though it's none of my business," she said, "you might take a lesson from that ol' dame. So," she said, shifting the topic, "tell me how you convinced that young buck to drop his pants and model for you." Janice's blatant declaration made Keighley howl with laughter.

"Janice! What have I done?" Keighley's face turned beet red. She covered her face with her hands and laughed into her palms, bursting with embarrassment, excitement, and a terrifying new discovery.

"Sweetheart, you're doing everything just fine. A tumble in the sheets may be just what the good doctor ordered!"

"Oh, Janice! No. Do you think he … ? Oh no. Oh shoot. Oh no. What have I done?"

"What are you so scared of? Keighley, it's about time! You cannot continue to hide in that house of yours. It's turning into a prison and you've become the—"

"Wait a minute," Keighley interrupted. "Prison? It is not a prison. I've been taking care of my grandfather. It's not a sentence, Janice."

Janice paused a moment to regroup her thoughts. She replied softly, "It is when you stop living."

The words stung Keighley, but deep in her core, she knew Janice was right.

Keighley paused for a moment and let the words inhabit her. She took a breath and looked at her friend.

"So," Keighley asked, defeated. "What do I do?"

"You get that buck into your studio, watch him drop his trousers, load up your paints, and you paint his naked ass from here to Lighthouse Bay!" she laughed heartily and loud. It was infectious and Keighley, despite her fear, found herself laughing along.

"But what about Pop-Pop?" she asked.

"He'll be fine, trust me. Let the man alone for a minute. Send him to a movie with Mrs. Sylvane. Have some fun for yourself for a change."

"Yeah, I guess," she replied. "This guy is something else. Connor is so … Well. He's …" Once again, the words stuck in her throat.

"He's what?" Janice asked. "Honey, I see you. I see your face light up when you simply say his name. Say it." Janice smiled teasingly.

"Huh?"

"Say it."

"Say what?" Keighley was confused.

"His name! Say it."

"Janice, I,"

"No, child, that's not it. Say his name. Say it."

"If I … "

"No. Say it!"

"I … " Keighley stalled.

"Honey, now!"

"But, it's not …" Keighley was stumbling.

"What in heaven's name are you so afraid of?" Janice demanded.

The panic was building in Keighley's throat. "That he'll see me!" she shouted desperately.

"What are you talking about?" Janice replied, shocked at Keighley's revelation.

"That he'll see me, that way I live! What I gave up on. I'm a college dropout, a freaky fortune teller with the crazy grandfather Janice! The leaking roof, the sloppy yard, the broken shutters. That stupid Fortune Teller's sign! There's not enough cash for repairs except for a jar full of crazy pennies. All of it. The house, my job, my life. I'm a mess. I'm perfect material for that magazine. I live like a freak. What guy would want to be a part of that?" Keighley's outburst was loud and sprung deeply from her core.

Janice paused.

She let the transport pass and watched Keighley as her breath slowed down. Janice was relieved by Keighley's outburst. It was a long time in the making and finally saw the light of day.

"Honey," she said. "He's already seen all of it. He saw the house needs painting. He saw the crooked shutters, and the lawn and the pennies. He knows you're a palm reading waitress, too! He saw your Pop-Pop and his weakest point and he really came through. Remember? Seems to me not much scares this guy. And even better, he's coming back for more. And this time, he's dressed for the job." She paused and grinned naughtily. "Or undressed depending on the occasion."

Keighley looked at her friend, slightly embarrassed about the possibilities. "What am I going to do?"

Chapter 16

"A book? You want me to hold a book?" Connor's voice sounded a little incredulous. Nervous. "Who reads naked?"

Keighley let out a healthy laugh. "No, you nut," she teased, "It's not about the book. It's just a prop. It accentuates the lines, the angles, the light. Besides, it hides your hand and fingers are really hard to paint."

They were standing in Keighley's studio. The sun was just inching upon twilight's magical hour, filling her room with the hushed golden serenity typical of evenings in Cobweb Corners. The gentle rhythmic sound of the reassuring waves folded in the distance and a deep bell clanged from the bay. Ginger was curled up on an old throw, lazing in the warm light. Purring softly, she gave her approval of this new visitor.

The scent of oil paint mixed with the saline wings of an evening's ocean breeze was heady and intoxicating. Connor stood by the window, his naked body wrapped in a huge sheet. He was fumbling like a young man in his first suit, awkwardly trying to hide his insecurity, trying his best to ignore the bead of nervous sweat trickling down his side. Tickling his abdomen, it was evidence of his fear, proof of his apprehension.

"So? Now what? Do I just stand here?" he asked, fearful of her reply. He tried to sound calm and sure, yet his insides were screaming like a twelve-year-old's.

Keighley's voice came from behind her canvas. Was she hiding? The canvas was huge, about five feet tall by three or more feet wide. He could see the tracks of her large brush sweeping across the tight material as she primed the surface.

"Well, first," she said, "you need to drop the sheet, buddy-boy."

His reply was quiet. "Um, yeah," he managed to say.

Keighley poked her head around the canvas. "Connor," she said. "You're fine. Really. Just pretend you're in a locker room." And she disappeared behind the canvas wall again.

"There's a reason they don't allow female reporters in a locker room ya know." He laughed nervously.

She made a few final sweeps across the tight fabric. "Okay, almost ready," she said, still hidden behind her canvas. "I want to paint you from behind, so turn and face the window?"

He turned, like a little boy wrapped up in his mother's blanket. He took a deep breath and prayed his body would behave. Though feeling very excited, he knew his nerves would take care of suppressing any embarrassing developments below the waist.

"Now, really, time to drop the sheet buddy." She laughed at his shyness.

She heard a sigh.

A few shuffling scuffs as he turned.

The soft sound of a sheet unfettered, falling like velvet on freshly fallen snow.

The distant drone of rocking waves gently enveloped the room.

The air was still.

Keighley took a quiet step from behind the safety of her wall and looked at this man. He was ready. He stood about ten feet away. His back was to her and the tight muscles in his back and shoulders stood out like sculpted bronze, highlighting his body in a sure and masculine frame. She could tell he was nervous, tense, tight. She stepped toward him and tried to reassure his nerves as she repositioned his arms.

"Okay, perfect," she said, trying to sound professional. "Now, I want you to hold the book, open, in your left hand, down by your side." As she tried to position his arm he interrupted her.

"Yeah, like I'm just an average naked reader guy," he joked, trying to relax.

Keighley laughed. "Connor, it's not about the book." She tried to position his tense arm. It was tense and wouldn't budge an inch. "Let go of your arm," she said. She shook it softly, attempted to position it by his side as naturally as possible. "Connor, relax," she coaxed.

"Not. A. Chance," he replied.

She laughed and shook her head. "Look. I want to paint somebody who looks relaxed and calm. You look like your insides are going to battle!"

"Oh man," he replied. "You don't know the half of it!"

They both laughed heartily. Ginger lifted her head, awakened by their noise. She lazily stepped from her nest of warm blankets, gave a stretch and sauntered across the room and out the studio door, in search of more silent spaces.

Connor noticed his reflection in the large window facing him. He shook his head slightly at the absurdity of the situation he found himself in. Modeling? Nude? Really? Him?

Keighley watched him, enjoying his humor, his shyness, his good natured ability. And the view. Especially the view.

She attempted again. "Okay, book at your side, relax the arm," she said. He followed the instructions. "Now, the right arm. Can you raise it? Hand behind your head like a big yawn?"

"Like I'm waking up?"

"Yeah! Good! Like a big stretch."

Connor did as he was asked. Positioning his hand behind his head created what Keighley intended. It flexed the muscle structure along his shoulder, along his biceps, stretched his neck muscles, and tilted his head slightly to the left, curving his finely chiseled torso.

"Perfect," she said. "That's it."

"So it's a painting of a yawning naked reader guy who just woke up?" Connor joked.

"Yeah, Connor," she replied, "and next it's going to be a painting of a naked yawning reader guy on a crowded fishing pier if you don't behave."

"Aw c'mon!" he teased. "This is scary stuff! Nobody, and I mean *nobody* knows I'm doing this."

Keighley returned to her canvas to begin choosing her colors. "What about your bucket list? I thought everyone had posing nude for a painting on their bucket list," she said as she squeezed out thick ropes of titanium white, naples yellow, french ultramarine.

"Bucket list? The words naked and bucket list should never appear in the same sentence," he said. "So how long do I stand like this?"

"About a year," she teased easily.

"What?" he shouted, and shocked, he turned to face her, forgetting his nudity, his vulnerability, and their eyes met.

They held each other's faces for mere seconds, locked in a gaze where time was meaningless. In that moment, they both knew joy. Connor smiled and Keighley saw him relax. A true breath entered his lungs and his armor dropped to his feet.

"You're doing good Connor. Now, how about we begin?"

He took one more look at her glowing face, her hair, her radiance, and succumbing to her request, he turned to face the window once more, happily employed under the gaze of this magical woman.

She began to sketch. He heard, but could not see, her gift of capturing light and life in all its true essence. He listened to the music of her long, broad strokes, the brush sweeping across the canvass like a soft wind over a field of wheat.

This could do, he thought, for a day, a week, a life—and he smiled inside of his exposed skin, wholly and full.

For nearly an hour, Keighley's arm flew over her canvas, sight followed by instinct, she quickly became enrapt in her task. Happy to have a model once again—working from life was always her favorite. The palette became alive as color mixed with medium, hues softened and sang as her brush swept through piles of flesh tones, ambers and umbers, glowing lights and dusted shadows, all flew across her canvas as she captured the strong lines of light reflected on muscle and contemplated the mysterious shadows of this perfect man's form.

This perfect man.

She stopped painting.

This perfect man, she thought. She stepped away from her canvas and gazed upon Connor as he stood there, innocently receiving her gaze, unaware of her eyes as they traveled across his defined shoulders. His biceps stretched his bronzed skin tighter than her canvas. She was warmed by the view. She noticed how the shadow below his biceps highlighted the form of his arm as it arched over and above his shoulder. Dark against light, muscle contracting against the softness of his skin. Warm umber richness against a male tawny glow.

"I'm doing okay?" he asked. "Sounds like you stopped painting."

A muffled meow answered from down the hall.

"You're fine," she responded. "Just looking at the light, figuring, you know."

Her eyes traveled across his right shoulder to the center of his shoulder blades and lingered there, like honey poured on silk. They traveled down the strong path of his spine, touching each vertebra until she landed upon his hips. The round curves of his muscular buttocks formed a welcoming contrast to the hard strength of his back. She smiled. His shoulders, hips and buttocks tapered to a taut triangle and defined what every artist sought since the beginning of time. Perfect form, perfect symmetry, and the balance of muscle against skin, light reflected from form, and the curious space where function meets desire.

"Well?" he asked. "Did you stop? Can I turn around now?"

"Not just yet," she replied. This view was too fantastic. Suddenly, all artistic integrity about painting nudes flew out the window and Keighley gazed upon Connor. Innocent and perfect, she was relieved he couldn't see her. She gazed across his hips, journeyed over his strong and defined buttocks, dimpled at the hips, joining his thighs like iron on steel. His legs were covered in dark downy hair. Muscled like a wolf, as inviting as a dare.

"Umm, Keighley?"

"Yeah?"

"I think you should know," he said gently. "I can see your reflection in the window. What cha looking at?" he teased. He had been watching her all along, enjoying being on the receiving end of her gaze and desire.

She let out a guffaw of pure embarrassment and doubled over, laughing into her hands, shamed at having been caught, loving his teasing approach and sought a place to hide.

"Connor! I'm … I'm so sorry!" She quickly leapt behind her canvas wall, hoping to hide her glowing red cheeks, burning from embarrassment.

He poked his face around her canvas like a disembodied head. A smile growing across his lips wider than the Nile. "May I come in?" he teased.

She blushed. Her eyes peered over her hands, glowing, welcoming, wet from being caught, wide in anticipation and joy. He appeared on her side of the canvas, sheet wrapped around his shoulders like a makeshift toga, appearing adorably vulnerable and powerfully Romanesque, all at the same time.

He lifted her chin on two of his strong fingers and held her eyes. "You are so amazing," he said softly, like a whisper through pines. "Who are you?" He searched deeply in her eyes for some answer, a light of recognition. "What is it about you?"

Ginger answered from somewhere above, meowing a few notes in a loud reply.

"Yeah! I think so too!" he said.

Keighley felt like she was being bathed in his gaze, washed clean and free of all previous apprehensions. The fear slid from her body and puddled at her feet. The old oaken floor happily absorbed it, and carried it away to distant corners.

"Connor," she said, holding his strong eyes, "if you don't kiss me now, I may pass out."

He laughed. Relieved by her spirit, encouraged by her words, he could barely find words. "I've never met anyone like you," he said. His heart was beating rapidly and he feared he may lose the battle with himself under the sheet.

He held her chin and stepped closer to her. She felt the warm air permeating around his solid frame. In anticipation, she took a quick breath.

"What's wrong?" he asked. "The artist isn't scared, is she?"

"Oh man," she replied softly, "you don't know the half of it."

Connor laughed heartily, recognizing his own words. "Well," he said, "that makes two of us."

His lips were full and warm and when Keighley felt the tip of his tongue ignited by the rasp of his slight whisker, the years of isolation flew away and she welcomed this man into her soul. Her lungs held him inside of her the way cotton absorbs the warmth of the sun, and she bathed in its heat. Welcoming the fire, she fanned the flame and leaned into Connor's chest, happily relying on his strong arms to support her years of suppressed desire, happy to have discovered it once more.

Ginger meowed again, somewhere above them. Loudly, urgently. Was it in response to this new man encroaching on her territory? A reply to the new discovery? A mouse? She howled again.

"Ignore her," Keighley mumbled, lost in the arms of desire.

"Um," he said between minute tastes of her delicious lips, "is she okay? Sounds like something's wrong …"

"No, no," she said, running her hands between sheet and flesh. "It's okay …" Keighley was inhaling his kisses, trying to fill up the lost space of her life, absent of kisses, holding in his mysterious scent of inner earth, copper and sea salt. Filling herself abundantly, she slowly pushed against Connor, locked in an awkward dance while trying to maneuver him toward the studio bed.

Another howl. Longer and deeper, Ginger's guttural notes bordered on panic. Keighley stopped, jarred back to life. She pulled away a moment and listened. "That's not right," she said. "Ginger howls, but not like that."

They listened.

A low growl, deep and threatening emanated from a space above them.

The attic.

Keighley sighed, but knew what she had to do.

"Connor, something's wrong. Wait here. Let me just check on her?"

"Where would I go? I'm not exactly dressed for a night out," he teased.

A loud howl pierced through the air, and Keighley ran out the door. "Connor," she yelled over her shoulder, "follow me." And she was gone.

With a wilted shrug, Connor dropped the sheet, tossed on his jeans and T-shirt and followed Keighley's voice out the door and down the darkened hall.

Chapter 17

She ran down the hallway as Ginger continued her deep howls against the unknown foe. Keighley ran around the corner and followed the hall to the rear of the house where the air became darker. The sun had set and the single window at the rear of the hall was lost in shadows.

Keighley noticed that the attic door stood open about a foot.

"Ginger?" she called. "Hey girl! You up there?"

There was no response.

"Connor? I think something's wrong," she yelled down the hall.

"I'm on my way!" Keighley heard Connor stumbling down the hall, clumsily attempting to finish dressing as he pursued her. He rounded the corner, jeans hastily fastened, hopping on one foot, quickly shoving the final sock over his bare foot held tightly in his grasp.

"What's going on?" he asked.

They both looked up the darkened attic staircase. The steps were old, dry, and sharp as peanut shells.

"You have your cell phone?" she asked. "Let me have it? There's no electricity up there and I'm not about to hunt for a flashlight."

Connor whipped out his smart phone, turned it on, and hit the flashlight app. The phone suddenly bathed the space in a cold sterile light. Its square shape glowed like a science fiction credit card. Keighley aimed the phone up the steep attic stairs. Its unnatural light reached about six feet in front of them. Beyond that faded into a deep, velvet darkness.

"Ginger?" she called gently.

Silence.

"Be careful on the steps," she warned Connor. "I haven't been up here in years, and parts of the floor aren't even finished."

They walked up the dusty stairs. Slowly at first, unsure the ancient tread and risers could withstand their trespasses, Keighley cringed at each creak and moan as the steps cried under their weight.

Upon reaching the top, Keighley let out a small laugh.

"Connor," she said. "Do you realize we've both been holding our breath?"

He laughed with her, relieved she noticed it first.

"I know," he said, happy to a knowledge his apprehension. "I feel like we're out of Scooby Snacks and Farmer Joe is right around the corner."

"Don't laugh, he just may be," Keighley joked. "We're in my house after all. Who knows what lurks up here."

A muffled meow replied, somewhere to the left, lost in the shadows.

"Ginger? C'mon girl" Keighley called softly and slowly swept the phone's light across the attic floor toward the plaintive meow.

Connor muttered softly, in awe of the space in which he found himself.

The light was insufficient, yet enough to reveal a huge dark space, deep and tall as a cathedral. The attic covered the entire top floor of the house and its angular gables appeared to be wings of lost time. Each gabled space held a tall, narrow window that reflected nothing but the silvery twilight outside and the blue reflection of the cell light held trapped inside its aged glass. The roof, made of ancient lathe and cedar, was supported by rafters and beams as wrinkled as dry carrot sticks, the discarded tooth picks of an aged giant. The floor was cracked and uneven like a dried riverbed, baked by centuries of an unforgiving sun. In fact, the entire space gave the impression of a deep forest, absent of water, its dehydration petrifying the trees into spindles and splinters of shattered pine.

Another soft meow from the corner.

"Hey girl," Keighley called into the dark recesses. "Connor, wait here. The floor may be unsafe in spaces. I'll go get her."

Keighley stepped softly into the room, and walked gently toward the soft meows in the far end of the attic. Gently calling to Ginger, Keighley walked slowly and the floor creaked beneath her. Each footfall felt secretive. Each step was selected. Connor watched as Keighley walked through the space, until the light could no longer reach him and he became surrounded in darkness.

She reached the far end of the attic.

"Ginger?" she called. "Connor, I don't see her," she called over her shoulder.

"Hey Ginger! C'mon gal! You're interrupting the first date I've had in years!" he called into the dark.

The absurdity of the situation suddenly hit her and Keighley laughed. She bent over and laughed even harder. Crouching on the dusty attic floor, clutching the awkward light in her hands, her laughter filled the ancient space with life.

"What's so funny?" Connor asked.

Trying to catch her breath she yelled back though her tears, "This. Just, all this!" Her laughter started up and showed no signs of abating. It was triumphant and soon Connor found himself laughing along. "She probably just found a mouse or something." She was half crying and wiping the tears from her eyes. "And here we are, like Daphne and Shaggy, hunting for a clue!" She roared, and Connor's laughter grew, warm and rich.

They reveled in their joyful release, and though separated by the length of the room and acres of darkness, Keighley felt a closeness she had never experienced until tonight. Though he was hidden in the darkness, Keighley was thankful for this man.

"Connor?"

"Yeah?" His voice was muffled in the dark.

"Thank you," she said softly.

"Yeah? For what?"

"For all this. For putting up with this … My life, you're a good man."

The floor suddenly shifted and rocked and Keighley froze at the sound of ancient wood snapping like ice. "Oh—" she said.

"Did you feel that?" she called into the darkness. "Connor!"

"Oh God, yeah … Don't move!" he called back. "I'll come get you."

Another creak, a loud groan, a threatening quake like mighty beam giving up its fight with age. The floor was crying out and warning its occupant of its terrible weakness.

"No! Stay there!" she called and directed the light across floor to Connor. "I'm on my way—"

Then the world fell.

The floor disappeared beneath Keighley's feet. Shattered wood and crumbling pine fell as Keighley's weightless body dropped into darkness. She screamed for Connor, yet her voice was lost in the traffic of noise and her descent ended with a hard plummet onto a darkened base. A sickening thud followed by the sound of heavy beams slamming against solid floor.

"Randy!" Connor cried out from his panicked soul, and terrified, he leapt across the darkness to the void. "Randy! Where are you? Can you hear me?"

The floor was still creaking. The sounds of the lumber's release softened and silence was all that remained. Dust infected the air like a sand storm.

Connor didn't breathe. He called out once again and dropped to his knees. He inched his way across the floor, weary of its unpredictable weakness. He broke a sweat that began to soak his tee as he felt the old terror rising in his throat.

Oh God, oh no, he kept repeating to himself.

He swallowed hard, forcing the bile deep into the pit of his fear and called out "Keighley! Answer me! Keighley!"

A muffled moan replied.

"Keighley? Where are you! Are you okay?!" He inched along, and when he saw the space a few feet ahead, he dropped to his stomach and pulled himself to the edge. Coughing, he swiped his arm across his eyes.

Another moan from below, inarticulate, but living.

"Keighley!" He pulled himself the last few feet to the edge, his eyes blinded from the dust, shattered floorboards with edges like saw-toothed bone rose around his grasp.

"Connor? What hap—" A cough racked her throat.

Connor peered over the edge into the dark hole. The cell phone sat next to her. Its unnatural light revealed a cramped space of chaos. Keighley was sitting among shattered wood, lost in a storm of dust highlighted by the faint glow of the phone.

"Keighley, hold on! I'm coming to get you!"

She took a deep breath and slowly began to take inventory of her body. The fall had stunned her. Her back ached terribly, and she could feel the terrible compression in her spine, but as she began to move a bit, she gratefully acknowledged there were no broken bones. She coughed hard, and it hurt.

"Keighley! Answer me, are you okay!" he called to her.

"Yeah. I guess. I'm … What happened? Where am I?" She shook her head instigating another storm of dust and began to cough again.

"I'm coming down!" Connor called to her. He maneuvered his body around the shattered floor boards and twisted his legs into the dark hole. Like an expert Olympian, he grabbed on to a solid beam, tested it for its strength and decided to trust it. He tossed his lower half into the darkness as the dust blinded his eyes and shattered floor boards scraped against his chest.

"Keighley, I'm coming in," he called. Allowing his solid arms to hold his weight, he slowly lowered himself into the dark—legs dangling in the air. Holding on to a broken rafter, his powerful arms slowed his decent and he dropped the final yard into the room below. He landed with a solid thud and was at Keighley's side.

"Keighley, what happened? Are you all right?" His panicked voice rang from his heart.

"Connor," she asked, shaking the dust from her face, "who's Randy?"

Chapter 18

"What?" Connor shook his head trying to awaken from what must be a nightmare.

"Randy. You called me Randy," she replied.

"Later," he said, swallowing his fear and trying his best to ignore the question. "Are you okay? What the hell happened?" He felt her arms, brushed the hair from her face, searching for any bruises and cuts.

"Are you hurt?"

The warm concern in his voice struck Keighley.

She took a quick inventory of her body. "I think I'm okay" she said. "No broken bones so far." She got to her knees and took a deep breath. Trying not to cough, she asked, "Connor, where are we?"

"You mean you don't know?" His eyes widened.

She picked up the cell light and swept the small room with it.

"I've never seen this room before in my life," she said quietly.

The small cell phone's screen revealed a world that had been locked away for decades, an antique time capsule. Ghosts hung in the air and watched from the hole above them above as the dust softly settled around the stunned pair, like dry snow from centuries past.

Keighley and Connor didn't move. They slowly became accustomed to the dim and dusty light. Silently, their eyes swept over the secret space. About ten feet by twelve feet, the room appeared to have been locked away and forgotten.

Until now.

Dozens of paintings draped in layers of cobwebs and dust were stacked against every available space, stacked on the floor, leaning against the walls a dozen deep or hung like a spidery patchwork quilt, some as tall as Keighley, others as subtle as a sleeping kitten. Over time, some paintings had tilted to ghastly angles. Some had warped to distort their imprisoned, torqued images. And the walls themselves? They were lined with thousands of small, rotting cardboard tubes. About an inch in diameter, they were stacked floor to ceiling in unfathomable amounts. Like ancient insect casings, they gave the impression that the slightest breeze would annihilate their skins leaving their inhabitants exposed, raw and bare.

An old table with a framed photograph, dusty and indecipherable.

A door.

A gramophone.

And silence.

But what stunned them both was the large mirror directly in front of Keighley. Leaning against the wall, it reflected Keighley's hair, her soft chin, her blue dress and her life-affirming smile against a brilliant background.

The only problem was, Keighley wasn't wearing a blue dress and she certainly wasn't smiling right now.

"What is this place?" she asked softly as she crept toward the mirror.

Connor watched and held his breath.

When she reached out to stroke her reflection, the mirror did not reach back. It remained stagnant, frozen in time, bathing the room in her magnetic smile.

"Is this Oz?" she whispered, staring into her silently frozen reflection.

"Keighley, it's you … I think it's a portrait of you," Connor said, amazed by the beauty captured in the old canvas.

"It can't be," she replied. "I've never seen it before and my grandfather stopped painting years ago." Wiping away decades of dust from the portrait, she took a sharp breath.

"Connor," she said gently, her voice almost imperceptible. "It's my mom."

Chapter 19

"They're all paintings of my mom," Keighley whispered.

She flipped through stacks of them. Each canvas revealed a smile, a glance, a mischievous joy that Pop-Pop captured in his daughter. Keighley moved to another half dozen. She brushed away the cobwebs and saw her mother's history in oil, linen, and wistful strokes from a master's brush.

"I never knew she was so beautiful," she whispered, almost imperceptibly, like soft wind on glass.

Connor watched, still and silently absorbed in Keighley's discovery, torn between intruding on a private moment, and captivated to see such wonder in this magical woman's eyes.

Moving away a pile of smaller portraits, they gazed upon a large, unframed canvas. "He loved her so much. Connor, look at this." About five feet tall, it featured a young woman in a simple summer dress. She stood just off center, in what appeared to be an artist's studio.

Keighley's studio.

She was in slight profile as she faced the viewer. The room behind her was illuminated by a large window, softened by a sheer drape that protected her ethereal world from the burning light of a summer day. Though the room appeared to be cluttered with the tools of an artist, it never distracted from the heart of the painting: the woman herself. She gazed from the painting with the serenity of a mythical goddess, perpetually reminding the viewer that all is right in the world, or her corner of it at least.

Her gentle arms were by her side while her hands graced the curve of her stomach. Her slightly protruding stomach.

That explains the smile, Keighley thought.
She's pregnant.
Keighley knew it.
Pregnant with me.
They stared in meditative wonder. They never questioned how to get out of this secret space. Their discovery was too rich, too personal, too magical to leave this hushed sanctuary.

"Can we get some more light in here?" Connor crossed the floor, leaving soft tracks in the dust like tentative footfalls in an early snow. A deep window, hidden behind an ancient, papery cloth, offered a slight reprieve from the darkened room.

He tugged on the weathered blind, faded like an old onion skin, and it snapped with a sharp rattle, disturbing the silence and alarming them both. Its lightening ascent raised another cloud of dust thicker than the fug of a Havana cigar. Connor coughed and waved the dust away from his face. The window had not seen a cleansing shower of rain in decades. Covered with a thick growth of ivy, it was festooned with winding tendrils and spidery veins. Dark, splintered shadows instantly crawled across the floor in a damp green hue, the color of an underwater twilight, and bathed them in a feeble cool glow.

The window appeared recessed about a foot deep, perhaps more, lost among more oblong tubes, stacked five deep, reaching to the ceiling on both sides of the ancient window.

He looked closely at the paper tubes.

He reached out and picked one up. About four inches long and an inch wide, they were heavier than they appeared. The weight surprised him.

He looked at the end of the tube. His eyes grew large as he acknowledged their contents. A smile crept across his face. He looked around the room and smiled as he realized what surrounded them.

"Keighley, come over here," he said softly. "There's something you should see."

Keighley turned away from the stack of paintings she was exploring.

"Look at the walls," Connor suggested, "what are those tubes?"

Keighley crossed the room to where Connor was pointing.

The window did little to add the needed light. The glowing blue rectangle of the cell, swept along the floor to where Connor was standing. Scanning the wall, her light reflected something new. Shiny disks were embedded in those papery tubes. Hundreds of them. Small glints of copper and silver smiled back at her as she swept the walls with her light.

"Oh. My. God." She could barely breathe as the enormity struck her. She slowly turned around and her eyes circled the room, glancing from floor to ceiling, trying to comprehend the amount surrounding them both.

Coins. Thousands and thousands of wrapped coins. Pennies, nickels, dimes quarters, half dollars, all wrapped neatly in banker's coin tubes and stacked at least three deep, sometimes more. In some spots they reached the ceiling, other places they formed a monetary bench lining the secret room. Add a few pillows and you'd have a perfect miser's heaven, a vintage Fort Knox.

"Pop-Pop" Keighley whispered. "We found Pop-Pop's pennies."

"I think we found more than that," Connor laughed. "There must be a million bucks in here!"

"Connor, I have no idea where we are. I had no idea this room even existed. We've got to find Pop-Pop." Keighley crossed the room with a firm resolve to the single oak door. Momentarily fearful of what may lay behind it, she reached out and grasped the knob, curious where it lead. She ignored her shaking hand as the knob turned slowly.

Time stopped. Images became frozen snapshots, and sounds, sound bites.

A gentle click, the knob turned.

A soft creak, the latch relaxed.

… and the door was free from decades of its secret prison.

It swung open gently on silent hinges and the room was hushed.

Another wall.

That's all. Where a closet or a hallway should have been was a flat grey wall.

"It's a wall!" Panicked, she pounded on it. "Pop-Pop! It's me! Pop-Pop! We're stuck! Can you hear me? Pop-Pop!" She pounded some more.

"Let me see that," Connor said as he crossed the room. He ran his hands across the wall separating them from what lay beyond. It was dry and brittle beneath his calloused palms.

He pushed against it with both hands and felt it give a little.

He pushed harder with his shoulders and knew the old plasterboard would crumble under his strong fist.

"Keighley, I can break through this, no problem. We're okay. Do you want me to?"

"What other choice do we have?!" she asked.

"Well, there's the way we came in," he gently laughed as he glanced above.

"Not a chance! Pop-Pop!" she yelled, pounding on the wall. "Pop-Pop!"

"It's okay, I got it," he said, backing away from the plaster board wall, bracing himself for the break out. "Ya know," he said. "If this was a short story, there'd be a chained skeleton behind that wall."

"If there's a skeleton in there," she responded quickly, "it's every man for himself because I am climbing over you to get the hell out of here. Now do it!"

"Here goes!"

Connor threw his weight against the wall with a deep "Umphf!" His broad shoulder made contact with a powerful slam and the wall buckled under his strength. He backed away and inspected his effort. A large dent, over a foot, marred the wall.

"Not bad," he said, pleased with the result. This was total guy territory and he loved it.

Keighley watched. She knew Connor was getting into the rescuer role and she began enjoying the show.

"One more time, and umphf!" he grunted deeply as his weight made contact with the weakening wall once more.

The dent deepened significantly. A crack appeared in the plasterboard, giving proof to his ability and acknowledging their escape was near.

"Lookin' good," he said. "Now, one last punch and we may be through!"

Connor began to elbow the large dent with strong, muscular

strokes. With each powerful blast of his solid arm, the dust rose and the wall shook. Cracks splintered like an egg shell ready to burst.

"Almost. Got. It," he said. He gave the hole one last powerful punch and his fist was through. Plaster dust rose in clouds and covered his fist and shoulder. Desperately, he began pulling at the fragments, poking through the cracks, tossing shards of wall-papered plaster board to the floor.

"Keighley, give me your light?" he asked. "I want to see what's out there."

"Let me try?" she asked.

Connor stepped aside and Keighley slowly approached the broken wall. She held the small light up to the hole.

She recognized the wall paper on the other side. "I know where we are!" She leaned forward and reached through the hole, sweeping the light across the new space.

That's when she screamed.

Chapter 20

The old man's face appeared from the darkness. Terrified, his mouth yawned open as he watched the fist break through the wall. He was frozen while the hallway shook around him.

Secrets returning, sorrows breaking free. The space where he locked his heart away was crumbling before his eyes.

He heard his daughter's voice calling from somewhere beyond his scope.

Then pounding. Was it the walls? His breath? His heart?

"Pop-Pop!" she called.

Confused, Pop-Pop made his way up the endless staircase to face the darkness of the second floor hallway. Its maze of corners disarmed the old man.

Where to turn?

He heard it again, "Pop-Pop!"

"I'm coming child" he said, as he felt his way along the hall. Confused by the voice, distorted by the return of memories he hoped to hide.

That's when the walls began to move. The house shook. The arabesque wall paper seemed to dance in obscene patterns as the wall behind began to cough and crumble.

The memory returned. All of its sorrows and regrets flooded the old man, and he remembered.

Everything.

He froze.

The secret exploded and the walls became alive as a fist tore through and demanded attention. A light shone on his face and he knew he must acknowledge what he had been hiding for decades.

A broken heart. The regret of a lifetime. Memories of love locked away where no prying eye could ever see them again.

Until now.

He blinked in surprise as the light troubled his darkness.

He barely dared to whisper …

"Daughter?"

"Pop-Pop! It's me. Keighley! Move away from the wall, okay? We'll be out in a minute!"

Keighley stepped back from the wall and shouted, "We're breaking out, Pop-Pop!" With the skill of a martial artist, she raised her right leg and kicked through the wall. The remaining plaster board crumbled and snapped under her perfectly aimed blow. Dust rose and sang as fresh air found its way into the locked away room.

The wall was open.

Keighley stepped into the hallway, brushing her hair from her face. She quickly embraced her grandfather and tried to sooth his frightened eyes.

"Pop-Pop?" she asked gently, "Is there something you forgot to tell me?"

Carefully, the old man approached the hole in the wall. Connor stood back and let Albert peek into the room. Albert held onto the recessed door frame with a tentative hand and Keighley watched as her grandfather's eyes sweep across the hidden room.

He lingered a moment, smiled, and his voice sang softly, "There she is, my girl. My baby girl …"

Chapter 21

The scent of tea filled the room as Keighley poured a second cup for her grandfather. Curling wisps of chamomile and mint rose in the air as the house settled around them.

"So that's why you tried to tear through the wallpaper," Connor suggested respectably.

"I guess so," Albert replied, embarrassed by his actions. He felt a little ashamed too. What he had forgotten, the pain he had locked away. He was worn out from the collision of memories swirling through his mind, but happy to find relief in this moment. He stirred a drop of honey into his tea.

He looked softly at Keighley. "When your mother died, I just couldn't look at those paintings. My whole body hurt. The grief was too much to bear, so I locked them away. And I guess I just forgot about it. Time does funny things, my girl."

"And the money? Pop-Pop, there must be thousands of dollars in there." Keighley tried her best to sound calm, but she knew this discovery was beyond her scope.

Pop-Pop took a big sigh. He sipped his tea with a delicate breath, and smiled slightly. "What can I tell you? I'm a product of the Depression. Hate to say it kid, but I told you so." He laughed gently, relieved to finally breathe once more. "My dad always said to save pennies. If another Depression hit, their value couldn't go any lower. Nothing's lower than a penny, right? Crazy idea. He thought we'd be millionaires just by saving pennies." He shook his head slightly and smiled at the memory.

"Pop-Pop, I think he was right … " Keighley said. "So it wasn't just the penny jar in the hallway? You've been hiding this secret for years?"

"Well, child, your grandmother thought it was a nutty idea, but she never objected to the penny jar. What she didn't know was that I was also stacking away coins from each paycheck as well. Looks like it paid off!"

"So why the secret?" Keighley asked.

"Child," he said kindly, "our hearts were broken. The mind plays tricks and I needed to lock away those memories if I was going to heal. Our hearts broke on that winter night that took your folks away. I suddenly became a parent again. You were only a week old, a tiny little thing, and I didn't know how to grieve. We didn't have time."

He took a deep breath.

"We found ourselves lost and healing couldn't come fast enough. So, I stacked every painting that captured your mom into that room, and locked them away. We became so busy raising you, it just became easier to forget." He looked into his granddaughter's eyes. "You became the sunshine in this old house. You know that? You remember that? Remember what I used to call you … "

"Sunny Girl," she interrupted.

"Yeah, that's it. My Sunny Girl." He thought for a moment. "My Sunny Girl, sounds good to say that again." He proceeded slowly. "Child," he asked, "how about giving me some time alone? I'd like to spend the evening upstairs. There's someone I'm longing to see again."

Connor watched as the two held each other's eyes and he was thankful to bear witness to this moment, this reunion where past meets present and the future stretches out before them in fields of hope and serenity.

Chapter 22

"I had no idea that room even existed," Keighley said. "Really, that upstairs is like a maze. It's confusing enough as it is!" She took another sip of her wine, and leaned against Connor's kitchen sink. He lived in a small bungalow on the edge of the bay and they had just finished their first meal together in his place. "Half of those rooms up there are just storage rooms. They always creeped me out, so I never played up there as a kid."

"Good move." Connor laughed. "You open one wrong door and you're lost in Wonderland!"

"I think we found that door," she replied brightly. "I hope he's okay … "

"He's going to be fine," Connor reassured her. "He's a tough guy. He just needs to be alone. He's overwhelmed and wants to go through his things, his memories … Alone I guess. It's a great thing that you two are so close he can ask for that. You guys are really lucky. I've never had that. Ever." He gazed into his wine glass and swirled the wine around in a ruby whirlpool.

"What about Randy?" she asked gently. "What about her?"

He froze.

Connor didn't raise his eyes. "Yeah, about that …" he stammered.

"Connor, I fell through the floor and you yelled out 'Randy!' Who is this Randy?" Her voice sounded more demanding than she had intended.

"She, um …" He stopped. His eyes gazed deeply into the ruby depth of his wine. Words were beyond this story he knew he had to tell.

He took a deep breath, focused and said, "She was my wife." He raised his eyes to meet Keighley's.

She knit her brows. "Wife?" she asked, somewhat incredulous. "A wife? You were married? Where is she?" She tried to sound blasé, but knew her emotional reserve was reaching its limit. The day's events had exhausted her and her patience was evaporating quickly.

"So, let me get this straight. I fall through the floor, and you think of your wife?" Her power to control her voice was gone. She knew she sounded angry and regretted it. The world logic and control had disappeared when she fell through the floor.

"No, Keighley, it's not like that. It's … I just had … It came back too quickly." Frustrated at his failing words, Connor ran his hand through his hair and held onto his head, trying to keep each bursting thought tightly wrapped under his skull.

"Connor, what is it? What's going on? Are you still in love with her?"

"No! No, she's …" he took another deep breath and held it in his lungs for a moment. "She died. She's—She's dead." He let the breath out, slowly and methodically, like an exhale of smoke. He closed his eyes and knew he had to begin, but where?

He began.

"We got married too young. We both knew it. I was still in college, and she worked at a book store …"

Keighley watched Connor's face as he told his story. Each memory, each path was written in his eyes, on his mouth, on his brows as they knit and unfurled as the story unfolded though the deepening night. He told her about their first year together in a small apartment above a deli, the long hours, the tight budget. At times he'd smile a bit at some of the memories, other times, his eyes would shut down in troubled silence as he attempted to express the fate of his past.

"We both knew the marriage was in trouble," he said. "Money was tight, our schedules were completely different. We began arguing about stupid things. We even talked about a trial separation. Then, she … " He paused a minute and gulped some air, like a drowning man's last breath. "Then she became pregnant."

Keighley saw that his heartbeat was accelerating. His face looked terribly pained and she sought any kind of relief that she could offer.

"Connor, it's okay. You don't have to tell me this, really."

"No, um. I have to. It's just hard ya know?" Another breath. "I'm a writer and I'm supposed to be able to find words. But they aren't there." He swallowed hard. His voice was shallow and distant.

Keighley reached for the wine bottle. "Here," she offered, "have another glass?"

"No, thanks. I … Um. I have to get through this."

Keighley felt embarrassed. Inept. Her offer suddenly seemed insincere and too simple for what she knew was approaching.

"So, Randy was pregnant," he began. "Great, I thought. Just great. So! We decided to try and make things work. We went to a couples' counselor for a few months. Things improved a bit. She began to show." He broke off here, not sure how to begin the final chapter.

The wild horses in the depths of his memory returned and were impatient to break out. He knew he was powerless to contain them.

Keighley saw the trouble on Connor's face. She heard it in his voice. She braced a bit for she knew the fall was approaching.

"So. That winter we started doing things together more. Movies, weekends away at Afton pond up north, that kind of thing. One day, um …" He paused. "One day, the pond was frozen solid, ya know? It looked like a perfect mirror. So we went ice skating. She was only about three months pregnant. What did I know?" His voice shook. He held Keighley's eyes, searching for a sign of forgiveness, for comfort. He didn't want to continue.

Keighley stood near him, waiting for him to find the words, praying silently that his unbearable pain could find relief.

"I guess she went out too far," he said quietly. "I heard the sound first. Like a million mirrors shattering all around me." His breath came in short gasps. He looked into Keighley's eyes. "I never saw her go," he said quietly. "I screamed for her. I yelled, people came from out of nowhere. They were all around me." The story became fragmented, pieced together as he attempted to describe his shattered memory. "Suddenly they were holding me back, and sirens." He slowly nodded. "I remember sirens." He took a long pull of air. "I think I was bleeding. I was bleeding too," he said. "I must have fallen or something, I guess. I know I was screaming. I think I was in an ambulance. I guess I was. It's still pretty blurred."

He paused.

"She died that night. The ice … It …"

He looked up at Keighley, searching for a sign of recognition, a moment of loss and unbearable pain unified them both.

"Oh Connor," she managed to say, not recognizing that the tears on her face were her own. "Oh my Connor, my baby." Without action or reason, her arms were suddenly full of this strong man she had grown to love. His weight was full and heavy and hard. She felt him release the years of tension and pain as her neck received the wash of tears from his pained, hurting eyes.

"I never saw them go," he choked. "Both of them," he said gasping for breath. "I lost both of them." The words, muffled in her neck, were choked with pain and grief. Years of repression were emptied onto Keighley's shoulder. She let this man empty his grief into her for what seemed like an eternity of tears. She received it like a gift.

"Oh, Connor," she said softly, stroking his hair, his back, holding him tightly. Making sure he knew she could withstand the trial.

She felt him relax a bit. His breath simplified, softened.

"I'm, um. I'm sorry," he stammered as he attempted to pull away. She held him.

"For what?" She asked softly. "For being human?" She looked at him, and held his strong face in her hands. Tears traced down his face and dampened his stubbly cheeks.

She kissed his wet face, gently. One on each cheek. "Salty," she said simply. This man had known pain. "Salt from the dry well. Keeping everything in," she explained. Then, she did something remarkable.

She took his hand, clenched like a tight fist. Softly, she

stroked his tense fingers, his bruised knuckles, and they began
to unfurl, like a shy snail. "There," she said. She lifted his
palm to her lips and kissed the center of his hand, softly, like a
butterfly's wing. "See?" she said, "it's out. You can let it free."

His palm opened up and welcomed her healing kisses.

Chapter 23

They spent the next few hours talking, intimately and honestly, revealing the pains they had both traveled. They shared the bruises their lives had earned, the cuts that bled deeply, and their failed attempts to hide those injuries of the heart. In those magical hours, exposing their wounds through words and shared intimacies, they noticed that their scars began the slow process of healing.

Keighley felt free. Her life of holding other people's palms and giving herself to their comfort became a light. Her fear of insignificance evaporated and what was left was filled with the simplicity of grace and gratitude. She was thankful for this moment, for this man.

Connor discovered the ease of pure breath. When he emptied his heart on Keighley's shoulder, he found himself emptied of pain and guilt, held in the warm embrace of this magical woman. He wondered about the journey that led him into her healing arms. For the first time in years, he felt free, absolved of guilt. Only sorrow for the loss remained. Randy and the child became an easier loss to bear, like a stone in his pocket. He knew that stone would always remain, but the stone was smooth and was a part of him now. Exposed to the light, he could identify that stone, recognize it, and allow it to walk with him.

The night sky deepened and spread itself over Cobweb Corners. Like a watercolor canvas, the hues shifted and darkened as their conversation led deep into the night. When conversation paused, when words were no longer necessary, they sat complete and listened to the wave's rhythmic meditation. It became a new song, heard through new ears, fresh, alive and whole.

He stood and held her in his solid arms, safe and warm. "What is it about you?" he asked with wonder.

She smiled, shyly. "Me?" she asked in slight disbelief.

"Yeah, you. When I walked up to your house that first day, I never expected ... Well, I never expected you. You came to the door, and—" He laughed at the memory. "One look and I turned to putty."

She laid her forehead on his chest and laughed. "Oh Connor, you were so funny," she said. "The way you stammered on my porch, you looked like I was about to eat you alive."

He smiled broadly, proud to have been captivated by this beautiful gingerbread enchantress. "Then," he said grinning wider than the Cheshire cat, "I would have died the happiest man alive." He put his fingers under her chin and lifted her face to meet his own. "I never expected the fortune teller to be so beautiful," he whispered, "and not just those eyes, either, or this face." He gently stroked her cheek. He tapped her heart. "It's in here. I don't know what you've done, but I'm hooked. Whatever magic potion you've got, I want a lifetime supply."

His breath was warm and left her dizzy.

So, he kissed her. Finally and completely. He brushed her hair from her eyes and looked deeply into them and saw the mirror of love looking back, reflecting him, solid and serene. When his lips met hers, they were warm and full. His slight unshaven stubble thrilled her spirit and reminded her of the pleasures that would follow.

When they made love that night, her gift was the rain that ended the drought that had been his sorrows and loss. She was giving and free with her love. She took him by the hand and led him. He acknowledged her gift and followed. When she undressed for him, it was a motion of pure radiance. Done without performance or shame, it was the simple grace that is revealed in the spirit of true flesh. Connor suddenly found himself breathless, awakened in a new world of experiences. In the night that followed, she taught him that intimacy is more than body parts and actions. He unlearned everything that cold-hearted men had taught him and traveled this new path in the serene arms of this singular woman. Realigning what he had believed with what he was learning from her, was no longer a labor. It was elation. It became the climax of his soul and in that moment, they both cried out, joyfully and in gratitude.

So they slept.

And as they dreamed, the warmth of their bodies healed the bruised landscapes of their souls and a gentle morning sun rose upon another day.

Chapter 24

Keighley woke early. The morning breeze of New England air gently blew in through a window, scented with pine and damp earth. She smiled and curled into Connor's warmth. The cotton sheets soft and enveloping, she replayed images from the night. All limbs and flesh, his firm muscles and rigid strength, her abundance and secret folds. His caresses encompassed her, the magic softness of his mouth. She smiled broadly and softly ran her fingers along the inside of her arm, enjoying the tingles of gooseflesh and her rising desire.

Connor was still asleep, lost in a world untouched by pain, the serenity that only slumber offers. She looked softly at his sleeping face. His slight smile at the edge of his firm lips told her his dreams were pleasant and good. She looked at him and wondered about his painful past. How could he bear it? How could he stand the loss and even worse, the memories? She knew in her soul that this man was good, sincere and kind.

She smiled.

Carefully, she gently swung her legs out of his bed. Coffee was the first thing on her mind. Well, coffee and a tooth brush. She looked around his bed room and tried hard to ignore the typical guy space. A tangle of clothes on the floor revealed the events from the night. A bra, a tee, a pair of boxers, pants and socks were ensnared in a complicated mound like the history of urgent lovers. A corner chair with a pair of jeans tossed like a discarded second skin, a few socks peeking out of a half open drawer.

She picked up his bathrobe that had been slung over the closet door and was suddenly enveloped in his warm heady scent. Wood, earthen—she never realized a guy's scent could be so comfortable and she pulled the robe's folds around her.

Tiptoeing into the hallway, the morning light revealed his bungalow to be a combination of masculinity and dorm room, a contradiction of the adult and the guy. Shadows from the rising sun darkened the deepest corners while the warm wood glowed softly. The ceiling fixtures from another century revealed a jewel box of architecture, yet the conglomeration of newspapers, magazines, and a suspiciously old pizza box told a different story.

She shook her head and smiled as she looked around. Resisting the urge to straighten up the clutter, she quietly peeked into what appeared to be his office. Light from two large windows illuminated the space of a writer hard at work. A large oak mission desk faced the door and was littered with evidence of a project under way. His computer was nearly lost behind a pile of books stacked like a precarious tower of Babel. Papers and journals, newspapers and magazines were tossed in random overlapping order like fall leaves lining autumnal roads. She stepped into the hushed room and approached his desk, the sacred writing space.

The books' spines caught her attention. Some appeared old and their ornate leather spines appeared out of place among the myriad of new paperbacks and library texts with their crisp, bold colors.

She picked one up. The cover revealed dated image of a gypsy gazing mysteriously into a crystal ball. *The Complete Gypsy Fortune Teller* the title declared in garish font, typical of the 1970s. She picked up another one, *Out Foxing the Fox Sisters*. She knit her brows in troubled surprise. She knew of the Fox sisters. Leah, Maggie and Kate practically began the mid-nineteenth century spiritualism craze, and for a while were the most famous women in New York. Maggie and Kate recanted their claims in 1888, died as frauds and were buried in a pauper's grave. It was a tragic tale, but why was Connor interested in them, she wondered.

The better to hear you with my dear …

She took a breath.

She picked up another book. *Spiritualism: Facts and Fakes,* it read. Research for his article she figured. But why were the books so caustic? So cynical in tone?

The better to see you with my dear …

Her heart beat accelerated a bit as she put the book down. Frowning, she moved to the front of his desk and saw much more. An article from the New York Times entitled *Fortune Tellers: Fortune Hunters* made her skin crawl. She shook her head in disbelief. What kind of article was Connor writing? She picked up a weighty, oversized book. Decorated with gaudy carnie posters of the bearded lady, the gypsy witch and Siamese twins, the title promised, *Parlor Tricks and Sideshow Freaks!*

Furious, Keighley dropped the book with disgust and with that slight bump, the computer screen sprung to life. Like Pandora's box, the bluish light spread through the room and the poisoned light drew Keighley closer. The computer's hum, a drone of sleeping bees, warned her of stepping too closely to this hive.

She leaned forward and read.

```
The Road Less Traveled—fake psychics—
[working title?] FORTUNE'S PARLOR, FORTUNE'S
FOOLS: THE SIDESHOW IS ALIVE AND WELL AND
LIVING IN NEW ENGLAND,

By Connor Jakes

Over the past five months, I have traveled
throughout New England, searching for the
best, home-grown psychics our nation has to
offer. I am proud to report that, though I
have failed to discover one true psychic, I
have experienced intimate freak shows that
can rival the tackiest carnivals the world
has to offer.
```

Keighley swallowed hard. She continued:

```
I sat in Madam Corelli's parlor, (choking
```

in her haze of mentholated cigarette smoke)
as she gazed into a crystal ball, listened
while Miss Lyngstrand made a fool of herself
with predictions of my past (she was wrong,
dead wrong), nearly died while choking on my
suppressed laughter as Madame Arcana invited
me with "Come into my parlor said the spider
to they fly." Really? Trying hard to ignore
the tacky beads that hung in the doorway, it
was even harder to ignore her crooked teeth
and smoker's breath.

What did I discover? Of the six independent,
self-proclaimed psychics I visited, all
were women, single (or divorced) worked
out of their homes (note to lawn care
professionals, you may want to make a
visit yourselves! It seems psychics have
something against mowing), and five out of
six had a healthy addiction to mentholated
cigarettes. Got a rainy afternoon to spare?
You'll discover the best of the New England
sideshow is alive and well in your own
backyard.

Fortune Teller #1: When I arrived at Madam
Corelli's, I was invited to sit at her table
and …

Keighley stopped reading. Frozen with disbelief, it was impossible to ignore the stone-heavy truth in front of her eyes.

Connor's article.

The better to eat you with my dear!

The wolf was at the door.

Connor.

She looked up at him and stared directly into his betraying eyes.

Waiting.

The moments seemed like hours as Connor's guilt grew on

his face. Pained, "Keighley, I ... " was all he could manage.

"Sideshow freaks!" She confronted him. "Really? That's what I am to you? A sideshow *freak*?"

She walked to where he stood, framed in the doorway. Pained by his guilt, he became the boy he was, a wolf no longer.

And she slapped him.

Hard.

"Did that hurt?" she asked.

His cheek reddened under the crack of her palm. Only his eyes could reply.

"How dare you." she whispered. She refused to cry.

Gathering all of her strength from the most remote corners of her wounded spirit, she pushed past the frozen man in the doorway. She walked into his bedroom and grabbed her discarded clothes, car keys and purse. She didn't bother getting changed.

"Keighley, please! I was never going to ... I couldn't!" He followed her. His voice was urgent and panicked. "You gotta listen to me," he begged.

"Save it, Connor. Really," she replied firmly. She walked into the hallway and paused by the door. Firming the bathrobe tie like a suit, she looked directly into his face.

"I feel sorry for you Connor. I really do. You're a coward and you refuse to see what's right in front of your face."

She turned to the door.

"It's poisoned," she said softly. "I'm leaving. Don't follow me. Please let me have that dignity, okay? If you want your robe back, it'll be in the ash pile behind my garden."

And with those quiet words, Keighley opened the door and calmly walked out.

He watched. Too ashamed to follow, he tried to call to her but the words choked in his throat. The lump, a solid rock made of guilt, shame, and the acidic taste of bile. He knew he should run to her, beg her not to leave, make her understand that he never finished the article. He couldn't once he met her. But he was frozen. Drowning once again. The old fearful terror had returned and this time, he had locked himself in and the wild horses were free.

"Keighley! Please!" he called to her.

Keighley got into her car and shut the door softly. She refused to give him the benefit of a raised voice or the sharp crack of a door slam.

She turned the key, and slowly pulled away. She saw his house receding in her mirror.

That's when she started to cry.

Chapter 25

Her bedroom became a retreat from daylight, phone calls, the cafe, and most of all, Pop-Pop's questioning eyes. Her eyes were red and swollen from three days of crying, three days of isolation. Silence and soft sheets became her world. Occasional, unfamiliar noises in the hallway broke the silence every now and then. Hammering, heavy footsteps, the shuffled awkward dance required when moving large objects. The muffled voices of men (the guys next door?) woke her each day. She knew it had to do with the secret room, the paintings, the money. The money! It was too much to think about. Then, add Connor's betrayal to the pile and her once quiet little world became overwhelming. So, she retreated and let the world take care of itself for a while.

This afternoon, sitting in bed, wrapped in volumes of cool sheets and hidden in a mountain of pillows, she scraped her spoon against the remains of a pint of Cheery Cherry ice cream and sneered at the stupid flavor. She was craving Vengeful Vanilla and Strangle Him Strawberry.

Instead, she looked at the empty cartons on the floor staring up at her with pictures of happy cows and dancing smiles. It all looked so stupid. Rainbow sprinkles rained over syrupy landscapes in a world where ice cream led to unadulterated happiness? What garbage. She scraped the last spoonful and tossed the empty carton on the floor where it spun for a moment and rolled next to yesterday's Banana Bandit and Walnuts. She slowly looked over the ice cream carton carnage on her floor. *Oh no.* How many cartons had she consumed over the past three days?

Frustrated, she sighed and snuggled deeper into her warm bed, pulling the sheets up to her chin. Ginger purred at the motion and got up. She stretched her rear legs, languidly, and with sleepy eyes, moved toward the sunny spot on the bed. Keighley reached out to scratch the sleepy cat's ear. The air felt cool on her arm. "My girl," she cooed softly, "my sweet girl."

Ginger hadn't left the bed since Keighley cocooned herself inside her bedroom and Keighley appreciated her old friend's constant company. As she stroked Ginger's silky coat, she stared into the distance, at no point in particular. For the hundredth time, replayed in her mind what happened with Connor. What went wrong? How could she fall for such a trick? Why didn't she see the clues?

What hurt her most of all was the simple fact that she felt so naive. For the first time in her life she let her guard down. She allowed someone into her quiet, protected world, and the wolves came running.

And she opened the door and invited him in.

Like Little Red Riding Hood, she ignored the advice and strayed from her path leaving her protective cape in tatters.

She let out a frustrated groan. "Ahhggg!" Angry, she pounded the bed with a tight fist. Momentarily disturbed, Ginger lifted her head, assessed the situation, and went back to sleep, with one eye peering through a heavy lid, just to make sure the sad woman in the bed was okay.

Keighley reached for a tissue, blew her nose, and tossed the tissue into the overflowing wastebasket. Her tears were subsiding, drowning in sugary oblivion. All that remained was the emptiness, and no amount of ice cream could fill that hole. Pop-Pop brought her trays of food and didn't press her for words. But still, he knew what had happened and he knew that when she was ready, she would talk.

Maybe she was getting ready.

She looked around the room. The sun was pouring in, as usual. Connor's bathrobe was slung over a corner chair, like a discarded lover, a badge from a broken heart, a souvenir too painful to burn and too loaded to keep.

So there it sat. Keighley was contemplating how to get rid of it when a knock came at her door.

"Keighley, sweetheart? It's me." The soft voice sounded motherly and familiar. "Mrs. Sylvane, honey. Can we talk?"

Before she could answer, the door opened gently and Mrs. Sylvane appeared with a lunch tray of chowder and a grilled cheese sandwich. "Oh my sweet heart," she said when she saw the disheveled room. Stepping over the empty cartons of ice cream, she asked gently, "What have you done here?" In a moment, the old woman was soon by her side. Placing the lunch on the bedside table, the kindly woman sat on the bed next to Keighley.

Keighley took a deep breath. "I don't know," she said softly, as of the sound of her voice would awaken the pain. She looked up at Mrs. Sylvane. "He was lying the whole time. I don't know what happened. How could I not see that? He thinks I'm a sideshow freak! And ..." She tried to continue, but when she saw the concern in the old woman's eyes, her tears began to fall once more.

Mrs. Sylvane pulled her into her arms and laid Keighley's head against her chest.

"Oh my poor baby," she cooed softly. "I know, I know." She rocked Keighley as the young woman cried against her, heavily. Keighley took gentle refuge in Mrs. Sylvane's comforting arms and poured her tears into the old woman's heart. "There there. I know. I know how it hurts. That's it ... Let it all out."

So she cried against the woman's shoulder, a soft shudder every now and then, and when she felt the tears subsiding, she pulled away. Searching for a tissue, she said, "I must look a mess," she mumbled softly. "I haven't showered in three days."

"It's okay. I know right where you are. Truly I do." Gently, Mrs. Sylvane continued, "You've guided me through some painful days, you know that. I'm here for you, you know I am." She brushed the hair away from Keighley's face. She approached the next subject delicately. "That young man has been calling and calling, everyday."

"No!" she said instantly. "That guy has no business here. Ever."

"Keighley, child, he sounds mighty awful." Attempting to

end the conversation, Keighley got up to leave. "Now hold on there." Mrs. Sylvane stopped her. "Just you wait a moment. I didn't say you had to talk with him, and I don't know what happened, any of it." Her voice was reassuring and firm. "All I'm telling you is he stopped by yesterday morning. Seems he had a long talk with your Pop-Pop. That's all."

Keighley's face became rigid, like stone. "He has no business coming here," she said. "I'm fixing the gate by the road and he can pound until his fists bleed. He's not stepping foot into my life, again … Ever."

"You can do that, child." Mrs. Sylvane was pained to see the young hurt so badly. "You can lock the gate, lock the house up, even padlock that great big door of yours. But child," she paused, "don't you dare lock up that heart of yours. It's the only thing that has kept me going these past few years. Like it or not, Keighley, people depend on you. No way around it. Your Pop-Pop and the fellas next door ask about you. Your customers miss you and your tea. Even Janice down at the cafe has been calling. You're a part of the living, child. No escaping that. It's time."

Keighley listened to the words. They resounded with light. It was a dim light, but it was warm and nurturing and she knew that brightness could follow.

"I brought you some lunch. Eat up child, okay? You need more in you than ice cream." Her voice was warm and kind. Keighley knew this is what having a mother must be like. "Now, after you eat, I want you to shower? Okay? You look a mess. No telling what a fresh shower can do for the spirit! Use some pretty shampoo, too—that good girlie stuff." She laughed and touched Keighley's cheek.

Keighley smiled.

"Atta girl! There's that pretty face I know so dearly! When you're ready, I want you to come down stairs. Your Pop-Pop has something he wants to show you."

"Pop-Pop!" Keighley shouted, suddenly aware that she had neglected him for three days.

"He's fine, he's fine," Mrs. Sylvane reassured her. "I've been here, the boys next door have been helping. There's quite a find in that room you discovered. They've been helping your grandfather. They even brought dinner over last night. What a cute couple they are. And that tall one, mighty fine cook, too! We even played canasta." She laughed a little, and then paused a moment. "Life goes on, my girl. No matter how we try to hold on, it only spins forward. You have a good heart my Keighley. A good heart …" She got up from the bed and crossed to Keighley's door. "Now, eat your lunch and hop into that shower. Then, go downstairs. Your Pop-Pop has been worried sick, and it's time to join the living, okay? Besides, I made a fresh pound cake with homemade peach preserves."

And with that, she was gone.

Keighley took a spoonful of the rich chowder. She smiled as it warmed her tongue.

It was time to join the living.

Chapter 26

Keighley stood in the downstairs hallway. Her damp, freshly showered hair hung down over her clean cotton summer dress. She stood silently and looked around the hall. The hallway looked cleaner somehow, brighter. The air was abundant and the autumn tones in the wood were warmer and seemed richer too. The weight of the house, the dust, the dull wood work, the worn staircase bannister, all of it appeared to have been washed and polished with golden honey. She felt like she had stepped through the looking glass. Was she still in her home?

She turned toward the front doorway. The sun reflected in new patterns off of the floor and bathed the hall in amber. Even the massive penny jar behind her had been washed and now it shined like a magical aquarium, filled with gleaming copper pennies that seemed to smile against the ancient rippled glass.

That's when she noticed the hallway wall. The paintings had been changed and rearranged. At least half of them were paintings she had never seen before; well, until the discovery of the locked away room. The old paintings she was so familiar with seemed fresher among the new discoveries. She saw them through new eyes and for the first time in years, she felt the sense of wonder return. Her life, Pop-Pop's … her parents.

New paintings of the herb garden out back made her see the past with wonder and delight. Not just the physicality of the garden, the placements and the pathways, what we think we see. Instead, Pop-Pop's brush captured the very feeling of the space itself. The elemental unseen-ness of the eternal growth, the fecund soil cool beneath the vibrancy of physical life. It was a marvel to see.

The large canvas of Hattie in bed, which gave Connor such a start, now hung in the direct center of the wall, no longer lost in the shadows at the far end. Illuminated by light, it fairly glowed with life. Next to it was a painting she discovered three days ago: the mysteriously beautiful painting of Keighley's mom, young, hopeful, and pregnant.

It was difficult to take in. Who was the magician who revitalized this space so perfectly? She felt like she was in a new wing, a museum of freshly discovered art as she gazed at the unfamiliar paintings. They were pages from her history book, which had been missing for nearly twenty-six years.

She took her time.

Her bare feet were warmed against the sunlit oak floor, smooth from a thousand footsteps. She slowly walked the length of this great wall. Her dancing women painting, which won her a scholarship for her senior year, now hung at the front of the hallway. A place of prestige. It seemed a beacon, a welcoming in its new position, and she smiled.

Next to it was a portrait of her grandmother, Hattie, looking very young, mid-twenties? She held a bright child to her chest who was happily eating the remains of a vanilla cupcake. Her mom? The whole painting was done in swirls of yellows and whites, cream tones and ivory. Latte hues danced with vanilla as light radiated through the canvas. It threatened, joyfully, to spill over the frame and drip onto Keighley's bare toes. Keighley briefly wished it would. She would dip her toes into that magical puddle of light and she knew it would feel like joy.

She looked more closely. Hattie's head was tilted back and a large smile bloomed across her face. The sound of laughter that emanated from the painting filled the silent hallway and suddenly Keighley became aware of what life must have been like in this old house when Pop-Pop and Hattie began their family.

"Grandma," she whispered. She reached out and with the back of her fingertips, she softly stroked Hattie's young cheek. "You were so beautiful. I never knew … " For a moment, Keighley regretted the lives she never knew. The lives of her grandparents when they were young and filled with the potential of hope, their own child. Her parents, too. She saw their pictures, their faces in photographs, but somehow never asked questions that now, she would like to know. The sound of her mom's voice, the arms of her father, their dreams. Did they have silly pet names for each other? Did they embrace on the old staircase? Butterfly kisses?

The photographs she had were as silent as the dead. Frozen smiles, eyes caught half-shut in black and white shades of lawn-mower summers and snow-shovel winters.

She moved softly to the large portrait of her mother near the center of the hallway. She looked deeply into her mother's eyes for a sign of welcoming, of recognition, of *hello my daughter*.

She stood a long time.

"Oh mama," she said, tightening to refuse the tears that lay just beyond. "What am I going to do?" she whispered to the silent colors. For the first time in her life, she felt incapable to do what her journey demanded of her. How could she keep it all together? How can she bare the weight of regrets against the shattered possibilities. Upon discovering Connor's real motivations, her ability to trust herself suffered a terrible blow.

She wanted to share the weight with someone, but Pop-Pop? It would hurt him too much. She wanted to be strong for him, always. She thought of Janice and her offer for more hours at the cafe. Maybe she would take that extra shift. The money would help, it would get her out of the house more, and she needed some of Janice's strength right now. The idea revived her a bit.

"What do you think of the new gallery, Sunshine Girl?"

The rich voice startled her in the silent hall. She turned.

Pop-Pop.

"Who did all this? When? It's ... um ..."

"I'm glad you're out of bed. I figured, pretty soon, I'd have to force you downstairs," he said with a relieved smile hidden in his eyes. "But Ruth said, 'No, no, let the girl be.'" He paused a moment. "It's hard seeing someone you love hurt like that and not know how to heal it, not know how to help."

Keighley stayed silent for a moment.

"The guys next door brought the ice cream. Jonathan and Gary. They've helped a lot."

He waited for Keighley to reply. She nodded. Still silent. Too many questions were rolling in her head and she didn't know where to begin. Too many emotions that she couldn't identify—they were all too new.

"But you gotta watch that Gary at Canasta. He may be short, but he plays a hell of a game!" He paused. "Ruth and I played them last night. Did you know he and Jonathan are married?"

Keighley laughed softly. "Yeah, Pop-Pop," she said. "I know."

"Huh," he replied. "I never knew. Seems like I should have noticed that. They helped me a lot around here the past few days. I'm surprised we didn't bother you. All that noise, hammering and such."

He was hoping she'd take the bait. Wanting her to ask questions, yet fearful of pushing her away too quickly.

She saw it. His eyes held hers, and she knew he wanted to talk.

She began gently. "Pop-Pop, that room …? How come you never told me? Why were all of these paintings hidden in there? And the … "

"Let's sit here, Sunshine. I want you to meet your mother."

He sat down on the hallway bench and gently pulled Keighley down next to him. He held her hands in his weathered grip. Looking up at the large portrait he told her, "That was the last painting I ever did of your mother. She was about four months pregnant, with you," he added, as though Keighley didn't know. "She was something else, your mom. When she became pregnant, it was like a whole new world opened up for her. She was, well—electric! When your grandmother was pregnant, she was tired a lot, but not your mom. No sir! She wanted to try eating everything, go places, swim, hike … Ya know, she felt more comfortable outside than in." He paused a moment.

"Huh," he said, remembering a long forgotten image. "Isn't that funny. I'm just remembering that. She even wanted to sleep outside that summer. So Hattie and I bought your folks a tent and they slept outside for weeks." He laughed softly at the memory of the backyard tent. "That lady next door, Mrs. Katz, well, she just thought we were plain nuts!"

"You're a lot like her, you know?" he asked softly. "Maybe I never told you that enough, but there are moments when you smile, when you look at something deeply, and I know you see joy in it, you look like her. Like how you looked at that young man."

She stopped him, "Pop-Pop, no. Not yet."

"I want to tell you something child." He shifted his weight on the bench and settled in for what looked like was going to be a long story. "I'm glad we're here. Hattie is right in front of us. She's with us, ya know? And your mom, your folks. Well—" He sighed a bit and for a moment his grip tightened on Keighley's hand.

"The day we lost your folks," he said, "was the day my life ended. I didn't understand, child, how this could happen. We went from our life of … of joy and this, um … " He tried to use his hands to describe the immense, undefinable emotion, "Light and everything—*everything* was fine and Hattie was there, and your folks were there and we were happy."

He slowed down a little and continued. "Then, all of a sudden I was grieving my daughter, our daughter. Our light. Our future. Her husband—your daddy. Such a fine man." He paused to remember. "He fit right in, a son to us. He really was. Gone, just gone. Next thing I knew, I was holding you in my arms trying to figure out how to recover and protect you too. We didn't even have a moment to grieve. How do you love and grieve at the same time?" he asked. "Not enough room. No sir. Couldn't fit it all together." He took a deep breath.

"So," he continued, "I had to choose, we both did, me and Hattie. I couldn't live with the past anymore. It just hurt too much, child."

Keighley noticed his breath was a bit more shallow and heard the soft tears in his voice. She held his trembling hand and let him continue.

"I couldn't look at the pictures anymore, I just couldn't. Same with Hattie. She never said anything, but I noticed she kept her head down when she walked through this hallway. So, I took them down. One by one. Locked them away. Replaced them with simple paintings of the yard, the rooms …

Empty rooms. Nothing with people in them, nothing to make us remember. It was years before I could paint again."

"What made you start?"

"You. You did," he said. "When your mother died, I thought my life was over. I didn't want to hold you. I shut down. I drank a bit, too. I hid the paintings of your mother. One day, Hattie put you in my arms and said, 'Albert, your girl needs you. Love this child. You don't have to talk. You don't have to explain, but you do have to love. That's all we've got,' she told me. 'It has to be enough. It has to be.'"

He was quiet a moment, letting Hattie's voice reignite his efforts to help his granddaughter. "That's when I became alive again—discovering love. Child, I wish I could tell you how many times you have saved me. You had this look in your eyes. You still get it too! A mischievous look that lights up the whole world. People notice it, girl. They do! It's your strength. It's your resolve. It's your mom."

"Pop-Pop," she asked. "The money?"

"Oh that," he said with a note of slight shame and embarrassment. "It's age, my girl. Nothing more. I've always been a hound at saving my loose change. Used to drive your grandma nuts. I'm a child of the Depression. Must have got it from my folks," he said with a slight laugh. "When that penny jar became full, I just started stocking them away in the old linen room upstairs. No one ever used it. Hattie hadn't opened that door in ages. I figured when she found them, we'd have ourselves a nice dinner! The thing is, she never found them."

"Then, when I needed a place to hide your mama's paintings, I just stacked them in that linen room and decided to lock it way for good. But I kept going back to it. I'd walk by the door and my heart leapt each time I passed, as if your mama was really in there. Seeing the paintings stacked against the wall hurt. I wanted your mama so badly. I couldn't throw them away. Never. So, I just walled up the door. Took the temptation right out."

"What did grandma say? She just let you do it?"

"Yep, I got the plasterboard, the wallpaper, and went to work. She watched and didn't say a thing, but I knew what she was thinking. All along I knew."

"I finished the job, and just sat against the wall. Silent like, ya know?"

"Uh huh," Keighley said. She had never heard Albert talk so much and waited patiently for more.

"Hattie knelt beside me. 'Albert,' she said, 'We gotta finish burying our lives soon. Okay? I need you. The baby needs you. Your family misses this man,' she said and she tapped my chest, my heart I guess." He was quiet.

"Pop-Pop, I never knew. I'm so sorry," she tried to explain and knew words would be meaningless.

He smiled at her. "Sorry? For what? My Keighley girl, you got nothing to be sorry about. You brought the light back to me. See that painting there?" he pointed to the one with the cupcake. "That's want you gave me. You taught me to see again. You gave me my life back. Once I found it, there was no turning back. I couldn't go back. I locked everything away and let it be." He looked at her.

"I never knew time would pass so quickly," he said. "One day you're five and your face is covered in vanilla icing, laughing and the world was healing, next thing I know, you're in college and that room is lost in a dim memory. The house needs repair, child, don't think I haven't noticed. I've been foggy lately, the stroke, the medications, but I knew I had put money aside. I just couldn't remember where. I'm sorry about that. I know I scared you, but …"

"Pop-Pop, no. Never. You don't have to apologize for anything. I'm glad you're okay. I need you, Pop-Pop. Every day … Okay?"

He held her face in his calloused hands. "My Sunshine Girl," he said. "We're a good team. Your grandma would be proud."

"I know she would have. I miss her," Keighley said. "I'm glad you hung the paintings here. They're beautiful. You must have loved them so much," she said wistfully. "Pop-Pop, the money? What about that?" she asked gently.

"Well girl. The night you found the room was hard for me. I was embarrassed, and scared too. It was like, well … a door I wanted shut forever finally exploded. I had to face it, on my own. After a few hours, it was too much to bear, so I called

Ruth. She was there when, well, during the accident, and she remembers your mama, Hattie too. So I thought she could help me. We sorted through the paintings all night, laughed a bit too. I'm glad she was there."

"Pop-Pop, the money?"

"Right child, right. Well, there was too much of it there. We couldn't do anything about it. It was too heavy. So we called the guys next door, and Ruth and I had breakfast."

"Pop-Pop, the money? Where is it? Did you count it?"

"Good Lord Keighley, of course we didn't count it. Did you see that room? We'd been up most of the night, the guys suggested we get some sleep and get the process started in the morning. And that's what we did."

She nodded, impatiently waiting.

"Ruth and I stayed here, making sure you were okay, and sorting through that room while the guys went back and forth between the dropping off crates of coins at the bank, refilling your ice cream and making runs to the hardware store. For three days too! The guys did a real fine job repairing that old door. Hallway looks the same as it did a hundred years ago."

"Pop-Pop, are they counting the coins? How much is there?"

"Well child," he said, "seems like we did okay. There's a little over forty thousand and counting."

Keighley's eyes widened in surprise. "Forty thousand?" she asked. The words barely rolled off of her lips.

"That's what I'm told. Some old coins in there too, or so I hear," he said. "New roof, what do you say? A paint job. Get this house looking ship-shape again? Hattie would want that. I do too. New beginnings are everywhere you look," he said. "Even Ruth—she brought over these cushions," and he held up one of the bench cushions they were leaning against. Country-style ducks surrounding a red gingham center. It was just one of the new additions to the home. They were totally out of place, but they were made with love, so there they sat.

"Ruth? You two are on a first-name basis now?" Keighley asked, flirting for a bit more information.

"Keighley, Sunshine, haven't you seen the amount of peach preserves that woman drops off here? Haven't you noticed?

When a woman drops peaches on a man's porch, it's more than jelly. Where've ya been?" He winked, and began in earnest. "Now, I know you don't want to hear about it, but you need to listen. That young reporter man has been by here every day. He's been to the cafe talking off poor Janice's ear. He's tried to get the guys to get you messages upstairs, too. Now I know he may have done something bad, but you need to hear it from him."

Keighley tried to interrupt but Pop-Pop continued.

"No words about it. Keighley, you cannot run from heartbreak. I know that more than anyone here. I know you hurt, child. I know it, and it pains me. But you have to let that young man speak. He was here yesterday, and we had a long talk." He squeezed her hand tightly, protectively. "Now I know you don't to want to face him, so I heard him out, alone. Keighley girl, there ain't no other way around it. He told me what he did ... was going to do and I admit. It was real unkind. He made me mad, terribly so. But I listened, and child. I understand the guy. He never followed through with that story. How could he? He told me everything."

He paused a moment.

"He lost his family, he told me that," she responded.

He looked at Keighley and knew the words reached her. "Keighley, girl, that's a wound no one recovers from. Not quickly anyway. At least I had your grandmother, and you. That fella, his grief was his own. Grief can make you do mighty odd things. Sometimes, your judgment ain't right. What right did I have to lock away all those pictures of your mama? They should have been hung on the walls all over the place! You should have grown up with them so you could see what kind of a woman your mama was. It pained me to see them, to remember her, to know she was never coming back, so I locked them away. I was selfish, and losing your mama made me blind. I didn't know I was hurting you, or my Hattie. I knew I needed to heal, and I thought locking everything away would help."

"But Pop-Pop," she began. "He betrayed me! I trusted him and he wanted to make me look like a cheater, a liar. How could he? That's not a man I want around us."

"I know, child. He told me everything. He was blind. Stupid, and selfish. Most of all, he didn't know. He didn't know how special you were—*are*. But I think he knows now. He's got a good soul, Keighley. He does. Trouble is, it's lost somewhere in that hurt he's got. It happens to us all. We get lost in the sea of our own hurts. We drown in it. It's hard to see the light when you're in that deep. The path is gone and there's no air. And that boy is in … deep. But Keighley, he knows it, and that's a good thing. His door has been locked away too tightly. People crack in darkness like that. They do. Be the light, girl. Shine just a little bit of it on him so he can forgive himself. You don't have to like him, you don't have to see him afterward. But child, you do have to offer him that light of yours, just so he can find his way back to shore. Like I said, you don't have to like him."

"But Pop-Pop," she said slowly, "trouble is, I think I'm in love with him." She whispered the words sorrowfully.

"I know it, child. Now, you need to decide what to do with that."

And so Keighley began to talk. She opened up herself to her grandfather and revealed her hurts and fears. Sometimes tearful, sometimes laughing in recognition too. She talked a long time.

As she began to talk to this wise old man, the sun slowly traveled its warm journey across the sky, shadows falling in noon-lit heat. One ray, one golden-hued ray chose to reach through the lace curtain window of one particular home in Cobweb Corners. It rested upon a painting of a grey-haired woman, reclining in bed, whose magical flesh warmed under the new sun.

Her smile illuminated the room.

Chapter 27

She met him at the driveway gate the following day. The early morning air was crisp and wet. His hands were deep in his pockets. His blue jeans were thrown on in haste, white tee under a gray hoodie he quickly pulled from a hamper upon receiving her text. *Time to talk* was all it said. His heart pounded under his shirt, for he knew he would receive news of his fate.

Guilt, shame, sorrow, regret.

How can all of these emotions be contained in one man's body, yet still leave room for love? For he knew he was in love, deeply, with this magical woman and he knew he hurt her, terribly.

She arrived. Slowly walking across the yard, damp cold grass tickling her bare feet, she absorbed as much strength as she could muster to face Connor.

When she spotted him at the driveway entrance, he was turned away from her. She stopped for a moment and simply read his body. The signs on his body were as clear as the lines on his palm the first day she met him. She saw his hands were hidden, his shoulders were hunched, he paced. Fear, shame, anxiety, sorrow. This was not a man ready for battle.

"Mr. Jakes," she announced, her voice shook slightly. She wasn't prepared for the confrontation, but knew she had to face this man.

He turned, startled, and could only hold her eyes for a moment before breaking the contact. He looked away. "Keighley, let me—" he began.

"Connor, You betrayed me terribly," she interrupted. The hurt in her voice was palpable. "You came into my house, my home, and intended to make me look like a terrible person, a lair, a cheat and a thief. Right?"

He couldn't respond. The lump in his throat blocked language and held it like a cement stone in his stomach, hard, solid and cold.

"How could you?" she continued. She never yelled. She didn't demand. She confronted the betrayal as compassionately as possible, yet with the strength of a thousand women before her who, due to history, custom, or region, could not find a voice to confront the betraying man they faced.

Keighley found her voice and it was strong, healing, and good.

"Connor, my life may not be a typical life. But it's a good one. I'm a fortune teller, yes, a waitress, yes, a college drop-out. Yes. But I never claimed to be psychic. I told you the first time we met that I don't predict the future. You, yourself made up that part. All I do is see what people bring to me. And you, Sir, brought a cloud as black at pitch. Can't you see it?" she asked simply. "I saw it the moment you walked into my house. Didn't need your palm to see that."

"Keighley, I … " he tried, but couldn't get in.

"The worst part of it is, Connor, your words, that article, would have hurt my grandfather too. Didn't you think of that? Ever? Why would you do such a thing?"

She looked at his face, pained by the remorse she saw in his eyes, on his lips. The man hurt deeply. She could see that.

"Connor, I know you hurt. I know that. Both of us have lost a lot. Somewhere along the line, for some reason, we lost the people most important to us. I can't understand it, no one can." She paused, and tried to relax her arms, which had been tightly folded across her chest. "But what I don't understand, what I don't accept, is why you'd intentionally want to spread more sorrow? It just doesn't make sense to me and I don't want that in my life. Ever."

He looked up at her, braving her questioning eyes, and held them without saying a word. He knew she was right. He stood in front of her, exposed, raw, and for the first time in years, true.

"Now, Mr. Jakes, my grandfather says I need to listen to

you. I trust that man. Janice at the cafe tells me you've been in there looking for me as well. So? Why, Connor? Why did you come to me? Why are you seeking my friends? Was all this just part of your plan? Get the fake psychic chic? Connor, I gotta hand it to you, you got the article and you got laid. You won."

His head shot up quickly, "No! Keighley, no! You gotta believe me. It wasn't like that ... really." His voice was pleading, frightened and urgent. "I never meant to hurt you. Honestly, I didn't. I've never met anyone like you, and from the moment I left your home— That first day, I knew I wouldn't ...   I couldn't write that piece." He looked away from her, trying to keep his pain suppressed. He took a breath and looked deeply into her eyes, as gentle as a faun's. He silently pleaded with her to understand, to believe.

"Well then?" She asked.

He began. "Keighley, I would have never written that article, ever. I'm so sorry. I know how it hurt you." He was direct and his voice urged her to believe, to accept.

She stepped a few feet away from him and listened. Arms folded tightly, she protected her heart, yet listened with her instinctual goodness.

"Keighley, can we go somewhere? Sit somewhere so we can talk?"

"No. Connor, I've invited you into my home and you betrayed it. You can talk just as well right here as you can anywhere else. So spill."

She waited.

"Okay. It's when ... I took the job from Brian, when ..."

"Took?" she said incredulously. "Seems to me like you initiated it."

"Okay, yes. Just let me ..." Connor grabbed his forehead and tried to squeeze the words out, coherently, but the wild horses in his brain threatened to run wild and words were becoming a mess of stampeding hooves.

A deep breath, he closed his eyes. Another deep breath, and the horses calmed a bit.

"After Randy, um ..." He paused, unsure how to proceed.

"Connor, I'm sorry, you don't have to go there." She turned away slightly.

"No," he said and looked at Keighley. "I have it go there. It's where I come from, okay?"

"Yeah, okay," she said softly. She knew this journey was hard and discovered she was thankful to listen to him acknowledge his painful past.

"When Randy died, I … I choked. I stopped. I didn't leave the apartment for weeks, and I drank. A lot." He shook his head slightly at the memory. It was becoming remote. Was it really his life? "All I did was sit on that awful couch and watch TV. Remote in one hand, whiskey bottle in the other. Didn't see anybody." He paused and looked at the garden behind her. Its mysterious paths invited him in and he followed in thought. "Ya know, I can't even remember the funeral? I mean, yeah, I remember it, but it was like I wasn't there. Like I was under water or something." He shuddered at the sudden analogy. "Yeah, like I was underwater." He looked at Keighley. She understood.

"I had all of the shades down. The apartment was dark, and I guess, I tried to drown, too." The subtle flash of realization, the sudden light scared him for a moment and the words caught in his throat.

She saw how painful the memories were for him and resisted reaching out to help. This was a path he had to travel on his own.

"So, for months I locked myself away and lost—got lost, I guess. Never saw anyone. I was, um, I saw one of those TV shows, ya know? About talking to the dead? Some guy giving messages from the dead to people in the audience, and it just—I got pissed off. Really pissed off." He became a bit more agitated as he spoke. "I couldn't believe it. I mean, here I was, saw my wife and—and the, our, baby." He took a breath. "I saw them die and I couldn't do anything … *anything*."

His face began the painful process of releasing built up sorrows. With a strong swipe of his firm palm, he harshly wiped the few tears that gathered on his face and continued, determined to beat this thing, this weight that had drowned him for too long.

He continued, "And here's this clown saying, 'Oh it's all right. They're on the other side and they love you.'" His voice mocked the voice of the television medium. "'They love you and forgive you.' Bull! What bull!"

"So, you decided to get revenge?"

Her voice brought him back. Softly, he paused. He regrouped his words.

"No, it wasn't like that, not like that." A breath gave him more words. "Brian kept checking in on me. My only buddy who did. He offered me a spot in the magazine. Not that I needed the job. The life insurance policy took care of that, for a while at least. I moved. Bought the house, tried to make a new life. It was hard. It's hard."

"And the magazine?" she asked.

"I'm a writer Keighley. When I lost Randy, I ... Well, words didn't come like they used to. I have stacks of short stories, unfinished manuscripts, stories that just got stuck in me and can't get out. They're still stuck in me and sometimes I feel so full I could explode. I can't write fiction anymore. So, when Brian gave me the job, it was easier. The stories wrote themselves. A few months ago, I was in Walden's and that TV show came on again. The whole bar was watching it. Some guys were laughing, too. So, I thought about it and wanted to do something. So I started interviewing all of the psychics I could find."

"Like I said. Revenge?"

"Yeah," he acquiesced, a little beaten. "I guess so. Until I met you. That day, I knew the article was trashed. I couldn't do it. I wouldn't." He paused for a moment and looked at his hands. They were worn and beaten. But still, they had muscles, they were strong, and most of all, they were capable. "Keighley," he said, "I did something terrible. I got lost, ya know?"

She sighed, at ease. "Connor, I never claimed to be a psychic. Ever. I told you that the first time you walked into my house. All I do is read people. I'm intuitive that way. Everyone is."

He looked sincerely into her face. "Keighley, the moment I saw you, I knew that article was never getting written. I was scared. I didn't know how to approach you. I wanted to, believe me! I wanted to but I couldn't ask. It ... The words ... I couldn't find ..."

"So the interviews? What, they were like dates to you?" She

filled in the blanks for him.

A small smile appeared on the corner of his mouth. "Yeah. I guess they were. I couldn't get enough. My first date in two years. When I came back that next day? And saw you in the garden? I … I just stopped and watched you, you were so—"

"That's a little creepy," she responded quickly.

"No, not like that at all. You were in the garden and you looked like … Well … You were, um … Complete. Ya know? You were there, like you were whole, and you looked like you belonged there. It was the happiest thing I ever saw. I guess I wanted that. I thought if I watched you, I could learn how to do it, to get some of that too. To take home, so when I was alone, I wouldn't be so, well, alone."

Keighley looked at this guy, and for a long time they were both silent.

"Connor, why didn't you just tell me?" she asked simply.

"I couldn't. I'm scared Keighley! Don't you get it?"

"Connor, we all are. Look around you. Loss is everywhere! But you wanted to spread it! You wanted to destroy what little hope hurting people cling to. And who cares if it's a ghost! Who cares if it's a deck of cards, a crystal ball, a line on your hand? Connor, the world hurts. Every day. The best we can do is offer relief, solace, love and a little of compassion. We'd be fools otherwise! Spreading your cynicism will grow like a nightmare and evil people feed off of it. *That's not me!* Hell, half of the time I don't even charge for a reading! People come to me because they simply want someone, another human being, to know they hurt—or they're scared or lonely or whatever. That's all they want. We all want that. But you—"

He interrupted her quickly. "Keighley." He knew what he had to say and it scared him more than any loss he had ever lived through. He knew it, felt it, and knew instantly that it was time to let the wild horses free. Caged inside his head and heart for too long, they were hungry to live in the open once again.

He lifted his head and looked at her.

She returned the gaze, open, willing, and ready to receive.

"Keighley, I've fallen in love with you, and it terrifies me."

He smiled slightly. His face was tense and his jaw line was

firm. His eyes were actively searching hers for a sign of his fate.

She heard him and his fear released into the air that surrounded them. She smiled at him, and he warmed under her healing glow.

There are moments in New England when the morning air is so pure, it washes the soul clean. It's a breath that sweeps through the body the way a fine shower of spring rain purifies the maple and pine it falls upon, purifying the earth, renewing the soil and encouraging the tiniest seedling to seek the warmth of the sun.

She reached out and took his hand. Entranced, he responded, and followed her into the garden.

Chapter 28

" … add about three inches of that rich, organic mulch we talked about last week. Mound it around the base."

She demonstrated as she spoke. "And that should protect the rose from the harsh winter's snow."

Keighley smiled into the camera. She wiped her hands on her cotton apron as she stood. She finished with the cable show's well-known closing line, "And that's what's growing in your garden!"

The camera panned across the expanse of her fall garden. The days were much cooler now and the foliage surrounding the property was threatening to upstage her with a blaze of riotous fire tones, coppers and reds, oranges and yellows.

Highlighted by the newly painted house, she felt secure for the first time in her life. *It will look great on camera.* She knew, and she felt real proud of that. She smiled and waited for Brian's cue.

"Cut! That's a wrap," Brian shouted. "Another excellent show, Keighley."

Connor watched from the sidelines, proud of Keighley's success and relieved he was never on camera. She was a natural.

"Thanks, Brian," she said. "You guys hanging around for lunch this week? I know Ruth and Jonathan have been counting on it. They've been cooking all week."

"Absolutely. Only reason we film here," Brian joked. "Okay guys," he called to the production team. "Let's pack up—lunch time! Connor, dude, help me with loading the truck?"

The guys got to work and rolled up the cables that crossed

her garden like a growth of high-tech black ivy. Lights were disassembled, cameras packed, and clip boards disappeared as the crew restored her garden to its natural state of mulch-lined meandering paths.

Each week, Keighley's garden became the location for one of cable TV's fastest growing gardening programs called, *It's What's Growing*. Connor suggested the idea to Brian when he resigned from his position at *The Road Less Traveled*. Brian hemmed and hawed as expected, but when he met Keighley, he knew instantly that Connor was right. In more ways than one. They began filming in early August, and by October all of New England was tuning in on a weekly basis. Even Public Television was offering them a space.

Keighley watched as Connor hoisted the heavy cables over his solid shoulder and walked toward the trucks with Brian. How could she be so lucky? she wondered. When Connor suggested the idea for a gardening program, Keighley thought he was dreaming and dismissed the idea. It wasn't until she met Brian that the idea seemed possible.

She looked beyond the garden and saw they had begun preparations for lunch. Gary and Jonathan moved the large dining room table outside and put it next to the hemlock tree. The guys from the crew followed with an assortment of mismatched chairs. Ruth and Janice were setting the table with a feast. Janice brought chunky chowder, fried clams and lobster tails, hearty sandwiches and crab legs from the cafe. Ruth was slicing through an assortment of cheeses and crusty bread while Jonathan arranged a dozen candles and wild flowers around the table. Gary popped the cork on a bottle of white wine and smiled as he poured. Pop-Pop sat at the head of the table, a happy man, in the seat of a king watching over his extended family. He eyed Ruth's peach pie, knowing it would be the highlight of the meal while he stroked the big tabby cat asleep in his lap. Keighley smiled when she saw Ruth place a kiss firmly of Pop-Pop's cheek. He gleamed.

Joy. It was pure joy.

She twisted her engagement ring on her finger and a shiver of joy sprang through her body. Connor proposed to her on a late September afternoon on the requisite bended knee. Confident of her answer, he asked her on camera at the close of her seventh episode of *It's What's Growing*. Keighley was teaching her viewers about saving phlox seeds when Connor walked into the garden. She knew something was up. Connor never appeared on camera, plus he looked a bit more polished than usual. He wore a white Oxford shirt, neatly pressed, accentuating his firm biceps and solid shoulders. His usual jeans were replaced by khakis, but the biggest giveaway was the fact that he left his baseball cap behind. No cap? He looked stunning. Handsome and rugged, yet the shy guy still remained, about an inch below the pressed Oxford. His charm was deeper than the roots beneath her feet. She was thrown a little. His appearance wasn't on the outline for this week's episode. Pruning, seed heads, storing seeds: that was it.

"Keighley," he said, "I have a question for you." He got down on one knee.

Her heart skipped a beat and she noticed the cameras were still running.

"Since the first day I saw you, I knew you were magic. It wasn't until you began talking that I knew how magical you were. Like five seconds?" He laughed a little nervously. "I heard your voice and I knew. I never believed in love at first sight. I never believed in soul mates." His voice was shaking a little. "I never believed in magic—until you."

He took a deep breath and looked up at her, a smile growing across his face bigger than the tallest oak. "Babe, you taught me that magic exists. I see it in your garden," he said excitedly, "I see it in your art, but most of all, I see it in your eyes."

Keighley put her hands to her face, clasped, like a prayer to the universe, in thanks for sending this man to her. The tears that fell down her cheeks told Connor there was no doubt about her answer. Her eyes were shining like glowing diamonds.

"Keighley Woodson, whatever magic spell you have, I'd like a lifetime supply." He reached into the lavender growing on his right and pulled out a small oval box.

Keighley gasped.

"Babe, you are more beautiful than any flower growing in this garden. Be my wife?"

Connor slowly opened the small box to reveal a small

diamond flanked by two glistening amethysts, like faint purple leaves adorning a glistening heart.

He slid the ring on her finger. It fit perfectly.

And the show's ratings soared.

෧

Keighley smiled at the memory. It still thrilled her. She looked across the lawn and watched her friends gather around the large table. *Family*, she thought. *This is a family.*

She had never known such complete happiness.

"What cha lookin' at?" Connor's voice was warm and enveloping as he embraced her from behind.

She leaned back into him and surrendered to his embrace.

Their hearts found their rhythm and beat in unison. Words were no longer necessary.

"Connor, look," she said softly, wrapping herself tightly in his arms. They both looked at the group gathering at the table.

"Yeah, it's pretty great," he said.

She turned around in his arms. She faced him and looked deeply into him. She saw the reflection in his soft brown eyes, a reflection of adoration, connection, and honesty.

He smiled. *So this is what it's like,* he thought.

This man loved her. She knew that to be true. Her heart swelled as he held her and she knew their possibilities were as rich as the fertile soil beneath her feet.

"Babe," he said, "before I join you all, there's something I gotta do."

She smiled at him. "Sure," she said. "Don't be too long. You risk missing out on Ruth's pie." She kissed him on the cheek, the stubble, sharp and bristly, made her smile inwardly and reminded her of the adventures in store for her that night.

He watched her join the group. They cheered her arrival and the chatter rose on the crisp autumn air. Wine glasses were raised in an impromptu toast and the sound of hearty laughter filled the garden.

This is family, he thought happily, and turned toward the house.

෧

Connor sat at his desk and looked at his computer screen. The single line he typed looked intimidated by the vast empty space below it.

The Fortune Teller's Garden, a novel by Connor Jakes, it read.

He looked out of the second floor window. The lunch was going on joyfully. Plates were filled, chatter rose and fell, the crystal clink of a wine glass, and the sound of occasional laughter rang through the yard as the group enjoyed the communal feast and warm company. He looked forward to joining them soon.

He looked back at his blank computer screen and took a breath.

She sold hope ... he began, and smiled at the endless possibilities in store.

The End

ॐ

Frances DeleCourt Winters

Frances DeleCourt Winters teaches Victorian literature at a small university in Pennsylvania, and spends the summers in a mountain community in rural northern New Jersey. When not reading the most recent romance novel or writing creative fiction, Frances works on restoring a Victorian farmhouse from its skeletal stone foundation to its original gilded gingerbread trim.

ॐ